The Legend of Lakshmi Prasad

The People of Christian Paris

The Legend of Lakshmi Prasad

Twinkle Khanna

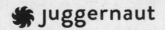

JUGGERNAUT BOOKS

KS House, 118 Shahpur Jat, New Delhi 110049, India

First published by Juggernaut Books 2016

ISBN 9789386228055

Typeset in Adobe Caslon Pro by R. Ajith Kumar, New Delhi

Printed at Manipal Technologies Ltd

For Akshay
Each time there is a power cut,
you, my friend, always have a flashlight handy

Contents

The Legend of Lakshmi Prasad   1

Salaam, Noni Appa   23

If the Weather Permits   77

The Sanitary Man from a Sacred Land 105

Acknowledgements   231

A Note on the Author   233

The Legend of
Lakshmi Prasad

Sandwiched between the river Kosi and the holiest of all rivers, the Ganga, there lies a village surrounded by thousands of trees. The foliage is so dense that it is difficult to see the rooftops of the small, brightly coloured houses that line up against the unpaved roads.

The trees all bear a precious fruit called jardalu, a golden mango so sweet that once eaten its taste lingers in your mouth for days, like a drizzle of scented sunshine. But it's not just its magical fruit trees that makes this village special. There's one thing even more remarkable about this place – it is the only village in the entire district where the birth of a girl child is celebrated with joy.

Once upon a time, though, this village used to be just like all the others – a brown, dusty land with small paddy fields, where boys were revered, while tiny baby girls were considered a burden and sometimes drowned in the river. Things changed because of a young girl and her name was Lakshmi Prasad.

~

'Ma! Take me also with you!' Lakshmi called out as she ran alongside the bullock cart. Surabhi Devi, Lakshmi's mother, was going to the nearby town to shop for Lakshmi's older sister Sukriti's wedding. She shooed her daughter away, her blue sari fluttering in the wind, and finally giving up, Lakshmi came to a halt on the dusty road and watched the bullock cart with her mother disappearing further and further away, towards Munger, a town that Lakshmi had heard so much about but had never visited.

It began to rain and Lakshmi walked back home briskly. Her yellow salwar kameez, already too short for her, was drenched and clung to her back. Her two pigtails, oiled and tied with black ribbons, were swinging in the wind as she began to run towards her house.

Her sister was sitting under the covered porch

with two of her friends and ignored Lakshmi as she walked by, aside from a perfunctory wave.

Sukriti never seemed to have time for her nowadays. The three-year age gap between the two sisters had not been a problem all these years when they played together, spending hours on the swing under the banyan tree by their house.

Lakshmi would sit on the swing, her sister standing behind her on the wooden plank, her salwar brushing against Lakshmi's back as they swung back and forth, the thick branch above creaking with their weight.

But now all of a sudden, Sukriti didn't have the inclination for what she called childish games. Wearing her mother's saris, she would sit with girls her own age, daydreaming and chattering about her upcoming wedding and her life ahead as a grown-up woman with a household of her own.

Lakshmi lay down on the mat spread out on the mud floor of her house. She looked around the room with its soot-darkened walls. One wall was taken up by utensils and the cooking hearth. On the other side stood a simple wooden shelf with idols of Brahma, the creator, Lakshmi, the goddess of wealth, and Saraswati, the goddess of wisdom. A red hyacinth flower and the stub of an incense stick decorated this simple altar.

She could hear snatches of the conversation on the porch interspersed with her sister's giggles. Feeling left out, she came out to the porch and sat at the other end, pretending to look away from the girls, into the rain.

Her sister and her friends lowered their voices, whispering among each other, and Lakshmi, now frustrated and bored, began to interrupt their conversation with random observations much to their annoyance.

She commented on a passing stray dog and the time a bee had stung Lachu, who lived next door. Hoping to show her sister's friends how close she still was to Sukriti, she said, 'Remember, Sukriti, we were playing langdi, and you got tired of catching me and we ate twelve whole mangoes and buried all the seeds in two holes with our sticky hands? Come, let's go and see if the seeds grew into saplings or not!'

Sukriti laughed condescendingly, wanting to let her friends know that she was infinitely more mature than her younger sister. 'Have you gone mad! It's raining so heavily and if mango trees grew in a few weeks then wouldn't everyone leave the paddy fields and grow mangoes instead? It takes years and years for a jardalu tree to grow and I don't know any fool who will water it every day and then wait for eight, nine years to get their reward, unless that silly fool is you!'

Lakshmi was stung by her sister's taunts – more so because she had been going to water the two mounds ever so often. No shoots had emerged yet but she had been hopeful.

Her eyes filled with tears. Determined not to let anyone see them, she replied defiantly, 'All right then, I am a fool and I won't have to water it now because look at the sky, all the gods are doing it for me!' Then she angrily walked out into the rain without any idea of where she was heading, leaving her sister and her friends tittering.

~

After Sukriti's wedding, Lakshmi started helping her mother more and more with the cooking, cleaning and washing – 'training for her future role as a homemaker', Surabhi Devi would say.

In the late afternoons she would take her father his lunch. Standing on the edge of the field, she would wave out till he saw her. He would then walk towards her, wiping his face with his stained cotton undershirt, hitching up his blue-and-white lungi as he climbed up the slope, his back already bent with age and fatigue. He would first take a long sip of water and then they would share chapattis with sliced onions and dal, crows hovering around them, waiting for their chance to get at a morsel or two.

Bijendra Prasad was very fond of his little daughter. He always told her that she reminded him of her grandmother. They had the same narrow hands and long face, the gap between the tip of the nose and the lips disproportionately large, but pleasing all the same.

On balmy afternoons, he would sit with her after lunch and tell her stories from the Ramayana. One day he told her about Shravan Kumar, who looked after his blind parents, spending his whole life serving them. Engrossed in the story, he murmured, 'That is why a son is so important, for his old parents to lean on. With daughters, all our life savings go away in giving and giving.'

Lakshmi, now sixteen, understood that he was talking about Sukriti and the intermittent demands by her in-laws in the last year for more dowry, or gifts as they called it. But she didn't ask him about it. Just at the mention of her sister's name, her father's mouth would tighten and he would rub his bony collarbone wearily and say, 'Sukriti is all right, everything is all right, it is manageable.'

Till the day it wasn't and a sunken-eyed Sukriti, her skin stretched like paper over each protruding rib, returned home, holding the gifts her in-laws had given her in return – burns on her back, from boiling water and hot pans.

Sukriti was back and as they also discovered a few months later, looking at her growing stomach, she had not come back alone. They sent news of her pregnancy to her husband in Tulsipur but no one came to take her back.

Lakshmi began accompanying her sister for long walks in the afternoons. Sukriti's bitterness brushed against her as they sat under the jardalu tree, squeezing the mango till it was soft, carefully biting the skin off one end and sucking the pulp, feeling the sweet juice trickling down their throats.

The seeds they had planted had grown into tall saplings but it would still be a few more years before they bore fruit.

Sukriti, her sari loosely draped over her stomach, her scarred back resting against the tree trunk, would often sigh, 'Lakshmi, I hope this baby is a boy. Life is easier for them. We girls have nothing. We go to live in other people's houses and they treat us like slaves. I would serve them food, and then whatever was left on their plates, I was meant to pile it all up and that was my dinner. A quarter chapatti from one plate, three spoons of rice from another, a single piece of cauliflower if I was fortunate.

'And the taunts would never end. "What did you bring from your house that we should treat you like a queen? Tell your father to send earrings for Diwali." Even my husband knew that he could kick me like a dog and I would crawl back with my head bent, willing to serve him again because there was nowhere else to go.'

Lakshmi looked at the branches filled with mangoes and asked her sister, 'Why can't we collect all these mangoes and sell them in the market like we sell paddy? Won't we get some money then?' Her sister replied, 'This is not our tree that we can collect the fruit and sell it!' To which Lakshmi said, 'But what if it were?'

Sukriti just shook her head. 'Stop daydreaming. This is just the way it is. But for my son, it will be different and with him in my arms I will go back to Tulsipur with my head held high. I already know what I will call him: Ramanand! Isn't it a nice name?'

~

Seasons changed. The monsoon unleashed its fury but, aside from a cow dying and their neighbour Ghanshyam's roof caving in, nothing momentous happened till the evening of Chhath puja. This was a big festival held in honour of the sun god and, as they did every year, Lakshmi and Surabhi Devi cleaned the house meticulously.

There were bananas to fry and sweets to be distributed. The entire village would gather that evening by the river and take dips in the twilight. The air would fill with laughter and music as the older women sang songs, beating a rolling pin against metal plates, a rhythmic drumming that kept time with racing heartbeats and the ritualistic dancing.

Surabhi Devi had finished making the thekuas, a sweet made of flour, jaggery and ghee, when Sukriti went into labour. Lakshmi sat on the porch outside with her father, hearing her sister's screams till she heard a baby cry.

She rushed inside. The room was filled with the stench of metallic blood and stale sweat. The midwife was holding the baby. She passed the baby to Surabhi Devi. After a long moment, Lakshmi's mother looked up and said, 'It's a girl.' The four women in the room were silent while the baby continued to wail.

For forty days, Sukriti stayed inside the house, her ears stuffed with cotton wool so that air did not find a way to enter her body and disrupt its already weakened state. These were village customs based on the principles of Ayurveda – a sari snugly tied around her stomach to help her womb contract, herbal paste applied on the soles of her feet so that heat would travel up into her chest and replenish her strength.

After a few weeks, Sukriti began to feel a little like her old self again. That's when her mother suggested that it was time for her to go back to her husband's house.

Lakshmi was taken aback. Was her mother really going to pretend that Sukriti had just returned home to give birth as was customary amongst most married women? But that was exactly what Surabhi Devi had been saying to everyone in the village. Her pride would not let her admit the sorry state of affairs.

Surabhi Devi spent hours talking to Sukriti, cajoling her, pleading that her husband would treat her well now that they had a child together and her mother-in-law would mend her ways. Sukriti soon started believing that things would truly change and was ready to go back to her marital home.

The journey, however, ended before it had begun. A few days later they received a message from Tulsipur. Sukriti's in-laws had heard about the baby girl and had washed their hands of the mother and child, claiming that Sukriti had not been pregnant when she left their house. This child was illegitimate, they said.

Lakshmi looked at her sister, who had collapsed on the mud floor in despair, her thin arms encircling her bent knees as she pressed her legs against her body. She stared emptily at the small hammock where her child lay fast asleep while her mother cried, 'What will we do now? What about Lakshmi? Who will marry her? We had nothing to give and now after this...'

Her father stood in a daze, a look of desperation seeping into his eyes. He said, 'I will sell the field, I can work as a day labourer. It doesn't matter. We will give the boy's side whatever they ask. We will manage.'

In all her seventeen years, Lakshmi had never felt such rage. A blinding rage where her heart thumped, her hands trembled, even her ears felt

14

like they were burning up with heat. In a quivering voice, barely in her control, Lakshmi said, 'Enough with this managing, of this bending. Ma, I am not getting married! Not till every girl in this village has something of her own. It's only when we have something that people will stop treating us like we are nothing.'

Lakshmi sat on the porch the entire night, an old shawl wrapped around her to keep her warm. Her father came out twice, trying to convince her to sleep, but she refused to move. The hours went by. Lakshmi stayed where she was, watching the waning moon in the cloudless night, hearing feral dogs barking in the distance.

She would fall asleep intermittently, her head drooping against the wooden balusters, only to wake up with a start again. She walked down from the porch just before dawn, her body stiff from sitting in the cold. She looked out at the village, the dusty road in front of her house, the empty stretch across, where once a long green snake had slithered over her foot, the banyan tree with her wooden swing swaying in the breeze. She cracked her stiff knuckles, stretching her fingers out, as she looked down at her hands, at her ten fingers. And then she found her answer.

Carefully cleaning her teeth with a neem twig, Lakshmi washed her face with a handful of water from the metal pitcher that she had filled yesterday. Holding her aluminium lota firmly in her hand, she walked to the fallow land behind her house and went through her morning ablutions, a singular notion spinning within the labyrinth of her mind.

She got back home to find the household awake, her sister feeding little Radha, her breast and the baby's head both covered with a yellow dupatta. Her mother peeled the ginger to add to the milk, cardamom, tea leaves and sugar boiling on the hearth. Her father, his sunken eyes unable to meet hers this morning, turned away, waving an incense stick in front of the clay gods.

When he finished his prayers, Lakshmi said, 'Babuji, will you come with me? Don't ask me anything, just come.'

Bijendra Prasad walked through the village, his daughter by his side. They were conscious of eyes curiously watching their long, purposeful strides. This was a place where people ambled; there was no need to hurry and there really was no place to go to either.

They reached the village centre and Lakshmi knocked on Shankar Singh's door. He opened the door and she began to speak, hesitantly at first, then faster and faster. The thoughts that had been locked inside her, and had probably been rattling in her subconscious mind for years, had finally been set free. Words falling, tripping, stumbling over each other, till she finally ran out of air. She took a deep breath, stilled herself and waited for his reaction.

Shankar Singh, at eighty-three, was the oldest man in the village. He was also the most respected as he had started the small school in the village and had taught simple arithmetic, reading and writing to the village children for generations.

He looked carefully at the tall, ungainly girl, in a black blouse that was too big for her and a green sari, both of which he was certain belonged to her mother. This little girl had thought of something that had not occurred to anyone in the hundred years that the village had existed. He asked her for time, time to absorb her ideas, and, most importantly, to convince all the people whose opinions mattered in this small community.

~

The jardalu tree was filled with fruit, each branch weighed down by half a dozen golden mangoes. Lakshmi had waited five months for this day – five long months in which Shankar Singh had gone from door to door to convince the villagers of her remarkable idea. She stood under the tree with him and her family, picked up makeshift cymbals made up of two metal plates and began slamming them together. Soon all the villagers gathered around the tree.

Lakshmi asked Sukriti to pass little Radha, her head covered in a pretty bonnet, a black spot on her forehead to ward off evil, to Surabhi Devi. The two sisters then used a long wooden stick and broke ten ripe mangoes off the tree, deftly using a knife to slice open the fruit.

They cut out the seeds, and planted each one

evenly in a straight row. Standing tall, eyes shining bright, she spoke solemnly: 'These ten trees are Radha's trees. They will grow along with her, taller and stronger with each year. When she is eight they will bear fruit. We will sell the fruit in Munger and that money will be hers. After that, every year her trees will bear fruit and the money will be saved for her, for her education, and for her marriage.

'Each time a daughter is born, we will celebrate and plant ten jardalu trees for her and they will belong to her forever. Ten trees like the ten fingers with which we women can hold our own destinies firmly in our hands.'

~

A schoolgirl is riding her bicycle on the narrow paved road towards the outskirts of the village; sweat drenches her uniform as she pedals furiously. Ruchira is late. She sees Badru, the old village barber, walking towards her and she calls out, 'Badru Chacha, what is the time?'

He takes out his mobile phone from the front

pocket of his cotton shirt and with a mouth full of betel leaves which have permanently stained his teeth orange calls out to her already receding back, 'Four-thirty! Go slow, Ruchira beti!'

She reaches the clearing. The ceremony has already begun. Colourful mats are spread out on the grass and on them women in bright saris sit with harmoniums and drums. She sees her friend Indu sitting next to her mother, the two red plastic tambourines lying in her lap, and quickly goes to take her place beside her.

The seven-day-old baby is in her mother's arms while her ten jardalu saplings are being planted into the ground. The baby's mother, Vidhi, has a bright smile on her tired face as she distributes sweets to everyone.

Ruchira watches the ceremony keenly, her fingers idly playing with the bells on the tambourine. She has her own ten trees in another spot closer to the village. On her fifteenth birthday, she will perform a simple ritual where she will tie a sacred red thread around each trunk, promising to look after them as they, in return, will look after her for the rest of her life.

Her mother had told her that this is the only village where people from any caste, even those with no land of their own, can plant trees for their daughters wherever they find space, even by the side of the road.

She wonders how this started – this ritual of the jardalu. But no one seems to quite remember, not even her grandmother, who says that this is just the way things have always been here.

The last sapling is planted and the women begin playing their instruments and singing a song about the benevolence of the great Lakshmi who blesses each woman in the village with happiness and prosperity.

It is an old song, passed down through generations and the women singing are unaware that the song is not about Goddess Lakshmi who resides in the heavens above, but alludes to a gangly girl who once walked among the mango groves.

Salaam, Noni Appa

An elderly woman popped her head out of the window of a dented white Fiat. It belonged to Noni Appa, who had just returned from Glory beauty parlour, which was why her carefully dyed brown hair was twisted around eleven rollers and covered with a pink net.

She called out to the watchman snoozing by the gate, 'Baburam, you duffer, open the gate.' Baburam, who seemed to spend as much time daydreaming as he did watching the creaky gate of Sea Breeze, shuffled forward and pushed the gate open.

Noni Appa, struggling with the shift stick, managed to push it into second gear and the car, moving like it was suffering from a bad bout of hiccups, inched forward towards the small house by the sea.

Noni Appa entered the weathered house and

spotted her younger sister, Binni, sitting at the dining table, drinking tea, peeling pine nuts and putting them in airtight containers.

Noni and Binni – these were not the names on their birth certificates. But over the years, whatever nice Ismaili names they had been bequeathed by the great Aga Khan himself had probably been wiped out of everyone's memories except theirs.

Binni was very animated this afternoon. She had received a parcel all the way from America. It contained two very important things – a videotape and a note.

She started prattling in Kutchi, their native tongue, a language similar to Sindhi, yet distinctly different. But her words literally and figuratively fell on deaf ears, as Noni Appa had as usual forgotten to switch on her hearing aid and had thus missed the volley of words though she had not missed the spectacle of her sixty-six-year-old, overweight sister bobbing her head up and down in excitement.

Noni Appa leisurely adjusted her hearing aid which had got tangled within the folds of her cotton dupatta and finally said, 'Koro thiyoh, Binni? What are you saying?'

Binni thrust the note under Noni Appa's nose. 'See this! Our second cousin Ibrahim, arrey, the Houston-wala, has spoken to someone in the Jamatkhana there. There's a nice Ismaili boy for your Mallika!'

Noni Appa sighed. 'Leave it, Binni. First of all Mallika is not going to leave London to move to Houston and, more importantly, she says that she is perfectly fine being single.'

Binni squealed. 'She is going to die a spinster at this rate. How old is she now, forty-six? Put this videotape in the VCR and at least see what a good match I have found for our Mallika.'

The room filled with the whirring sound of the video cassette player and then a wrinkled man wearing a striped shirt and grey pants appeared on the screen and said, 'Ya Ali Madad! My name is Shakeel Norani and I am a dentist.'

The image on the screen changed to different clips of him – in his office, beaming with a dental mirror in his hand, proudly pushing groceries in a trolley at a supermarket. The little show reel ended with him sitting in a car, his face contorted with passion as he lip-synced to an old ghazal by Mehdi Hassan.

Binni went on to explain, 'He has asked for Mallika's picture. Let's send it quickly, unlike other Ismaili boys he is very liberal-minded which is why he is accepting someone as old as her. In fact, before this he had proposed to Maneka, that film actress, but the foolish girl rejected his offer and married a doctor instead.'

Noni Appa snorted. 'Binni, this NRI dentist looks one year older than Allah Miya himself which means he must be the same age as you! Let's send him your photo. Just smile broadly in the picture and once he sees your three missing teeth, I am sure he will make a new set of dentures for you as a wedding gift!' And she removed the tape from the machine and thrust it back in her disgruntled sister's plump hands.

Noni Appa and Binni had both reached a stage in life where time had spiralled on to itself and, like their childhood days spent playing Dabba Eyes Spice in the by-lanes of Amreli, it was once again just the two of them against the world, having lost husbands to meningitis and cancer respectively and children to the lure of distant lands.

Noni Appa now filled her days helping out at Muskan, a school for special children, and her evenings meticulously writing duas into endless lined notebooks, while Binni, with money to spare and an empty bungalow where the windows rattled with both the sea air and loneliness, attempted to keep herself busy by constantly trying to find an appropriate hobby, often recruiting her elder sister as a companion cum guinea pig.

There had been art classes with poor Prahlad Bhai, where he kept trying to teach Binni to use a 2B pencil and sketch in grids and she, ignoring him, would jump directly to oil paints and canvas. There were cross-stitch classes which resulted in a piece of embroidery that proudly stated 'Home Seet Home'.

By the time the W had been reported missing by Mrs Mastan, who had been sitting right next to Binni, she had lost all interest in embroidery and was looking at Noni Appa across the table, signalling her that it was time to leave.

After that there had been singing classes, baking lessons and attempts at joining a laughter club. Binni and Noni Appa would walk to the beach dressed identically in printed salwar kurtas and gleaming white sneakers. They would stand in a circle with elderly gentlemen in a variety of caps perched on their balding heads, white shorts with socks pulled up to their knees, flailing their arms about while trying to laugh at nothing at all. And finally today, Binni had decided that it was time for them to try yoga.

The two sisters walked towards the garden. They were an incongruous pair. Noni Appa was shorter than her sister, frail and delicately boned, while Binni was well rounded. She had a large bosom and even larger hips, 'like a Coca-Cola bottle' as she liked to think of her formidable figure.

Binni called out to Bhondu, the cook and general dogsbody, to lay out three towels in the grass before the yoga teacher arrived. She told her sister, 'Take your rollers out. You look completely demented. And where are you going that you want to get all dolled up?' Noni Appa merely said, 'Is the teacher here to make me breathe in and out rhythmically or to pant over my beauty?'

Fifteen minutes later, they were sitting cross-legged on their towels in front of Anand ji, their new yoga teacher. Binni, who had once gone away for a seven-day vipassana retreat only to return in three days, was giving more instructions than the yoga teacher himself.

'Anand ji, tell Appa how to do kapalbhati properly, can't even see her stomach go in and out! See Noni Appa, like this, watch me.' And Binni, her entire body quivering, began violently inhaling and exhaling, while making pitiful bellowing sounds like an asthmatic buffalo.

Noni Appa ignored her as she continued her breathing exercises albeit while occasionally munching on pieces of papaya from a plate next to her as they sat facing their hapless yoga teacher.

Binni then insisted on performing a few asanas that she had circled in a book called *Tantra Kriya and Yoga* that she had purchased the previous week in anticipation of the imminent yoga session.

She decided to try the locust pose where she

was meant to lie down on her stomach and lift her legs alternately, but she had modified it by making Anand ji lift her leg and lower it for fifty counts.

She then slowly flipped over on to her back, wanting to do the pawanmuktasana, which could literally be translated as the wind-releasing pose, to alleviate her chronic constipation. The yoga teacher first pushed her bent right knee to her abdomen and then the left, a movement that was meant to internally massage the intestines.

Anand ji was now drenched in sweat, trying to push and pull Binni into some semblance of yogic poses. His white cotton kurta with buttons going up asymmetrically towards his left shoulder was sticking to his back and his thick grey hair was plastered to his head. The tall, elderly Gujarati gentleman was panting slightly as he repeatedly wiped his face with a handkerchief.

Noticing the yoga teacher breathing heavily, Binni snorted. 'Noni Appa, he tells us yoga means to breathe only through the nose and himself panting with mouth fully open, Kutho type. Practise yourself, Anand ji, and then teach us please.'

The class ended with both the sisters refusing to chant 'Om' – a sound that reverberates inside the skull like a noisy vacuum cleaner meant to suck away the garbage that the mind produces – with Binni adding, 'We are not lassi-drinking Hindus, you know?' So Anand ji settled for making them close their eyes and make a humming sound instead, like there was a bee trapped inside their mouths.

After Anand ji left, the two sisters had a quick discussion about him. Binni said, 'He was all right, nothing too great, Husna Ben recommended him like he was the great Patanjali himself.' And Noni Appa replied, 'I feel good, Binni, my muscles feel all pulled and stretched, like a ball of dough smoothened out into a nice flat chapatti.' Noni Appa then climbed into her white Fiat again and, with her foot constantly on the brake pad, carefully drove home.

She took the small elevator to her fourth-floor apartment in Juhu Scheme, unlocked the door and walked into her tiny apartment. She freshened up, removed her rollers, fluffing her mid-length hair into a wavy mass around her head, applied some maroon lipstick, changed into a grey sari and clasped a string of tiny yellowing pearls around her neck. She uncapped a bottle of whisky and poured some into two heavy crystal tumblers, topping each with cubes of ice.

Noni Appa leaned against the sliding windows and looked out at the towering gulmohar tree across the street, its branches laden with red flowers, moving in the breeze like blazing fireflies.

She glanced around the ramshackle, rather mouldy living room, at the peeling plaster and the ever-leaking roof of her home. She recalled entering this house as a new bride. The years of laughter when Farhan would urge her to slip into her imported chiffon saris, the same string of pearls dangling from her neck. He always wanted her to wear court shoes and not the Kolhapuri slippers that other women sported on their feet. The evenings spent sitting on the rattan chairs in the balcony outside, with a bottle of Black Label whisky and an ice bucket as she slowly acquired a taste for 'Scotch on the rocks' as he called it. Their daughter, Mallika, hanging a bird feeder on one side of the balcony and diligently filling it with grain and water for the parrots, sparrows and crows that flocked towards the tree-lined street.

She had dressed up for Farhan today, for what would have been their forty-eighth wedding anniversary. She looked at the black-and-white picture of her husband with his shy smile and his freckled nose, and placed the other glass of whisky in front of it on the mantel.

Clinking her own glass against it, she wished her dead husband a happy anniversary, wherever he was and in whichever form he existed, though his body was six feet under, in the large graveyard behind Galaxy theatre in Santacruz.

Noni Appa went out into the balcony and settled in one of the chairs. She sipped her drink, watching the colours of the gulmohar tree, all the green and red, change to a dark shadow against the night sky, as the sun began its journey to light up a day across some other distant land.

~

The next few days went by quickly, with Noni Appa spending more time than usual at Muskan.

The children were getting ready for their annual play, which would be staged in the first week of September. There were costumes to be stitched, intense negotiations with a seven-year-old who insisted that the cow she was meant to portray in the play should say 'mew' instead of 'moo' and a vegetable stamping art class, to make the stage background, where Noni Appa ended up with smudges of white paint on her blue linen dupatta. Then before she knew it, it was Thursday and she once again drove up to Binni's house for their second yoga class.

The house was deserted aside from Bhondu, who informed her, 'Binni Memsaab has gone with Shamim Didi to the market.'

'And what about the yoga class?' asked Noni Appa.

'I think there is class because she asked me to put out three towels in the garden before she left. Can I get you anything, Appa?'

Half an hour later, with two Glucose biscuits in her stomach and no sign of Binni, she was about to leave when she saw a rickshaw pulling up outside the gate and Anand ji walked in.

Anand ji peered at Noni Appa, who was sitting elegantly at the table with her wavy brown hair and pink lipstick, wearing a white cotton salwar kameez with embroidered blue flowers. She was a far cry from the creature he had seen at their last class, with her hair in rollers, trapped under the pink net like a captured hedgehog.

Noni Appa explained to the yoga teacher, 'Perhaps we should cancel today. Binni isn't home yet, though of course, Anand ji, you must charge us for the class as you have come all this way.' But Anand ji smiled. 'Mrs Machiwala, you are here, let's begin and Mrs Shroff can join us when she arrives.'

He placed his striped cloth bag on the small glass table to their left and then sat cross-legged on the towel, facing her.

They began stretching each joint, beginning at the toes. Noni Appa felt a flare of pain in her creaky right hip as they went along but soon that subsided as well.

Then they did some simple breathing exercises and finally Anand ji asked her to lie down with her eyes closed. 'Now we will begin the practice of yoga nidra. Make yourself comfortable. See that darkness in front of your eyes, it is called chidakasha, now as I say the words, try and see the same images in your chidakasha.

'The rising sun, a white lotus, a cloudy sky, a full moon,' Anand ji continued, throwing words at her till he finally asked her to rub her palms briskly, cup her eyes, open them gently and sit up.

Noni Appa did not move, so Anand ji repeated his instructions once again. He peered at her and thought that she had perhaps fallen asleep. He leaned over and clapped his hands sharply, right near her face, to wake her up.

Noni Appa opened her eyes with a start, and when Anand ji asked her if she had fallen asleep, she kept looking at him curiously. It was only a few minutes later that they both realized that Noni Appa's hearing aid had fallen out as she had shifted to a supine position and she had not heard a single word after 'Try to keep your mind blank as you lie down and close your eyes.'

'All this time I have been lying flat on the towel thinking that this is such a torturous experience. Hai Allah, the mind is also a strange thing, the minute someone asks you to keep the slate clean, squiggly lines of white chalk begin to appear, one line running into another in chaotic whirls,' she laughed, after firmly fixing her hearing aid and adjusting the small dial to get rid of a high-pitched drone.

They began discussing yoga and meditation as they stood up, with Anand ji explaining, 'That's what yoga is meant to do, bring order to that mental chaos.' Noni Appa walked towards the wrought iron chairs a few steps away and sat down heavily, feeling slightly dizzy. She suffered from low blood pressure and wanted a cup of tea. She didn't know if it was the milk or just the sugar but it always seemed to do the trick.

She called out to Bhondu and was surprised to see the other helper, Tito, open the French windows and come out into the garden. 'Arrey Tito, you are back, how are you feeling now?' Noni Appa asked. He had been with the family for over twenty years and had recently taken a few weeks off to go back to his village, complaining of pain in multiple joints. Tito replied, 'First class, Noni Appa, now I am fine.'

'Allah ka shukar hai!' said Noni Appa, asking him about his treatment. 'I went to a Baba in my village, Appa, he muttered some prayers and hit me a few times with his broom. Bas, in five days all sickness gone.'

Noni Appa shook her head incredulously and asked him to fetch some tea and a small snack. With a quick gesture, motioning Anand ji to sit down on the white chair, she said, 'I am going to tell Binni that next time she should just mutter a few choice curses and hit Tito with her vacuum cleaner, I am sure he will get better even quicker.'

Anand ji, a generous smile lighting up his face at Noni Appa's quip, protested, 'That may not work! He got better because he believes in prayers and his Baba, all mind over matter.'

Tito got the tea on a brightly polished silver tray, with floral teacups, white embroidered napkins and a plate filled with cucumber and tomato sandwiches. Noni Appa quickly drained her cup of tea and while Anand ji was getting ready to leave, dusting the crumbs of the cucumber sandwich off his kurta, she rummaged inside her cavernous grey handbag and pulled out a pack of cards.

She began laying them out on one side of the table, getting ready to play solitaire after Anand ji's departure. Noni Appa had decided to wait for her sister, preferring to have an early dinner with Binni instead of returning to her empty apartment and eating with her plate precariously balanced on her knees, as she flipped through old issues of *Femina* and *Reader's Digest* that she scoured from the numerous raddiwalas at Juhu market.

To her surprise, Anand ji leaned across the table and asked, 'Do you play little spider solitaire or the one where you reshuffle the deck?' Noni Appa looked up in surprise and asked, 'Do you play solitaire as well?' Anand ji nodded with a smile.

After retiring from his job in the Brihanmumbai Municipal Corporation's garden department he had found it increasingly difficult to adjust to being at home for most of the day. The three classes he taught, two in the morning and one in the evening, were the only respite from a home filled with the high-pitched squeals of his wife and the non-stop commotion caused by her relatives who kept walking through his door, like it was the revolving entrance of a motel. The incessant barking of his two small Lhasa apsos, Gulab and Jamun, added to this chorus.

For Anand ji, sitting by himself in the bedroom with a game of solitaire spread over the printed bed sheet, headphones plugged into his Walkman that invariably played Indian classical music as he hummed along, seemed the only way he could find refuge in his own home.

'Do you also play rummy?' asked Noni Appa. And Anand ji, who was reluctant to return to his noisy house as much as Noni Appa wanted to delay returning to her soundless one, nodded once more.

Noni Appa picked up the half-spread deck from the table, shuffled the cards and dealt thirteen cards each.

Under the slanting rays of the setting sun, they sat quietly, playing game after game on the rickety glass table in the middle of the overgrown garden crowded with coconut trees.

'Tu koro kaiyeti, what are you doing, Appa?' A nasal voice pierced the air. Binni was back, clutching two shopping bags from Kala Niketan, the sari shop next to Sahakari Bhandar.

Noni Appa shifted her glance from the cards gracefully fanned out in her right hand and said, 'I am reading tea leaves and predicting Anand ji's future. What do you think, Binni, playing rummy, you want to join in? And where were you all this time, you missed class also?'

Binni walked up to the table and frowned at her sister while breezily apologizing to Anand ji, who stood up at her approach, greeting her with a 'Namaste, Mrs Shroff'. Binni narrated a long-winded story about a dog and a bicycle and Shamim, none of which explained the sari-filled packets in her hand.

Anand ji merely said, 'Please telephone my house in the afternoons if there is any change in the class schedule,' and when Noni Appa bid both Binni and him to sit down so that they could finish the ongoing round of rummy, he played one last hand and got up to leave. Before Anand ji went, he said, 'Shubh ratri and do not forget to practise the first series of asanas before the next class on Monday.'

The two old ladies sat at the dinner table eating keema patties, a bowl of yellow dal without salt for Binni, who unlike her sister suffered from high blood pressure, a bowl of the regular variety for Noni Appa, along with rice and homemade mango pickle.

Noni Appa asked Bhondu for some sliced onions sprinkled with lime and red chilli powder and in between bites she said, 'You are eating mutton today, better remember to take your Kayam Churna tonight, otherwise you won't go to the bathroom for days on end and then you become so grumpy!'

Binni nodded and Noni Appa continued, 'Why did you miss Anand ji's class today? It normally takes you five sessions to get fed up of something. Do the yoga properly, Binni. Anand ji says all your stomach problems, blood pressure, everything will come under control.'

'You seem mighty impressed with that young fellow! Anand ji this and Anand ji that, playing cards with him also,' Binni teased.

Noni Appa shook her head. 'What nonsense

comes out of your mouth, Binni! First of all, he is sixty-three, which is hardly young and…'

Binni interrupted, 'But younger than you, Appa! And what you told me a few days ago about that dentist, wait…let me remember, yes! And you, Appa, are two years older than Allah Miya himself, so compared to you, he is a young fellow,' and seeing her sister quiet, she laughed triumphantly. 'Now what happened, you are not giving me any response only.'

Noni Appa looked at her sister affectionately, the right corner of her mouth twitching with a smile. Little Binni, she had always been like this – brash, brazen, flirtatious, teasing her more reserved elder sister, match-making her with dozens of boys who frequented the Jamatkhana when they were young, and once even with poor Peer Saab despite his snowy white beard.

Their life together had been filled with banter, silly jibes and jests, which tragedies, deaths and creaking bones had left unchanged. When she wrote duas in her book, she prayed for Binni's long life more than her own, because if not for her sister, her life would be an arid desert without any laughter-filled oasis.

~

By the time November gave way to a surprisingly cool December with the markets selling sweaters and shawls due to the unexpected cold wave, Noni Appa, Binni and the yoga teacher had slowly settled into a comfortable routine. Anand ji would arrive promptly every Monday and Thursday at four-thirty in the evening, though Binni would be missing half the time and threatened to discontinue every alternate class.

Her sister would then convince her, 'Get through this class first, Binni, then we will see about the rest.' They would finish their hour-long class and Noni Appa and Anand ji would play innumerable rounds of rummy, sitting at the glass table outside.

Sometimes Noni Appa would raid her sister's bar, calling out, 'Arrey Bhondu, one small whisky and three cubes of ice!' and at other times like Anand ji she too would be content with a fresh lime soda.

Binni, who found both cards and card players dreary, joined them only on the rare occasions that Danish Bhai, the video library fellow, was late in sending her video cassettes of her favourite Pakistani plays like *Buddha Ghar Pe Hai* and *Bakra Qiston Pe*.

Anand ji would leave around seven and Noni Appa would stay back at her sister's for an early dinner before getting into her dented car and slowly driving home.

~

In the first week of January, Mallika came to visit Noni Appa from London. She got her mother and aunt a suitcase filled with imported goodies: chocolates, perfume, hair dye and of course the one thing that every Indian woman pesters her NRI relatives for, undergarments from Marks and Spencer.

Binni eagerly took the coveted items from Mallika and dramatically declared, 'These British are really third-rate people, I tell you, their only saving grace lies in their first-rate bras. Their balcony-style Marks and Sparks gives such good support and pushes everything properly in place, straight from basement level to perfect third-floor height!'

That Friday, Binni dragged Mallika to the Jamatkhana, hoping some nice Ismaili boy would prostrate himself at her feet. In the car, Binni was chuckling away. 'Malla, you know, when your father passed away, Appa was not that old, just close to fifty. She would go to the Jamatkhana in her tightly draped sari and her pink lipstick...'

Noni Appa interrupted, 'Again this story, Binni! How many times!'

Binni laughed and ignoring her sister's protests continued, 'Arrey let me say what I want. Haan, so all the men in the Jamatkhana would look at her and keep trying to say "Ya Ali Madad" and then when they would go completely out of control, they would find sources to...'

Mallika giggled. 'What does out of control mean, Binni Masi? What would they do, explode in their pants?' And Noni Appa, horrified, almost banged into the autorickshaw that had suddenly halted in front of her.

'Chee, not dirty like that. They would send proposals, that's all, and after that your mother, always such a prude, with her constant "No Binni, I don't want to get a bad reputation" would never even greet them back,' said a giggling Binni. 'But I think things have changed, if you really want to know what out of control is, Malla, then you have to look at your mother. These days she is panting all over that yoga teacher, her boyfriend Anand ji!'

And imitating her sister with a wobbly falsetto voice, Binni continued, '"Anand ji, have a whisky today, the weather is perfect for it!" Turning that poor vegetarian Gujju bhai to an alcoholic, that also on my whisky.'

Mallika exclaimed, 'Mom, you didn't tell me all this!' Noni Appa, wanting to strangle her sister, said, 'Ya Allah! It is nothing like that. Yes, I offered him a drink and so sometimes he has one now when we play. Your masi hates cards so what should I do, just keep playing by myself?'

But the good-natured ribbing in the car didn't stop and, since Noni Appa could not turn her hearing aid off while driving, she just had to bear with her family, her eyebrows raised in exasperation, shaking her head at their sly digs.

That evening when the mother and daughter sat together in their balcony, Mallika asked, 'Mom, is this Anand ji thing really true? You can tell me, I won't get upset. Honestly, it will reassure me. As it is I worry about you being lonely here, how many times have I told you to come with me to London, but you never listen!'

Noni Appa shook her head. 'It is nothing like that, Binni talks nonsense! Is this any age to have boyfriends, you tell me? He is just a friend and it is nice to have some company rather than sitting by myself all the time. He likes playing cards. Sometimes he sings, he likes classical music, or he tells me about his days in the garden department and we talk about trees and plants, mealybug infestations and borer worms that attack trees, quite interesting really.'

Mallika leaped straight to what had caught her attention. 'He sings for you? That sounds very romantic!' Noni Appa laughed, 'To tell you the truth, Malla, he is actually a terrible singer.'

That night, long after Mallika had gone to sleep, Noni Appa lay tossing and turning in bed. She was filled with an uneasy feeling that she couldn't quite put her finger on. She felt a strange heaviness, as if something was lodged in her stomach.

She closed her eyes, deciding to try a meditative practice that Anand ji always claimed was an excellent remedy for insomnia. Noni Appa could hear his familiar voice in her head, telling her to relax every part of her body while visualizing a lotus at each chakra. But this time the soothing effects of the meditation eluded her, her mind playing tricks, replacing all the lotuses with images of Anand ji sitting cross-legged in the lotus pose instead.

Was the gentle, ever-smiling yoga teacher the cause of her discomfort? Had all her family's ribbing stirred up emotions that she had perhaps kept trapped inside her mind somewhere?

Noni Appa got out of bed, refusing to poke inside her head further. She felt her bloated stomach and decided that the only thing trapped inside her was probably wind. She boiled some water, adding ajwain to it, an old remedy for indigestion that she had learned from her mother. She sat on the sofa slowly sipping on her hot decoction, writing lines of duas meticulously in her book, waiting for the oblivion of sleep.

~

Mallika returned to her life in London, leaving Noni Appa feeling a little more desolate, the house a little more empty than it had been before her visit. She started spending more and more time with Anand ji. They would sit for hours around the glass table, the dark sky leaching away light, the cards in their hands growing dim, till they turned them face down on the table and started looking at the stars instead, exchanging stories in the dimly lit garden.

Innocuous stories at first. Anand ji telling her about his days at a hostel in Rishikesh: 'Soon I realized that a senior student, Swami Yogeshwar who was my immediate guru, was more interested in trying to teach me certain unnatural positions than the ones in the textbook. I took a train and came straight back to Bombay. Finished my teacher training course in Nashik.'

And Noni Appa telling him about the mischief

that she and Binni would be up to during their days in a boarding school in Pune: 'We climbed over every bathroom stall and locked it from inside. When the rest of the girls arrived, they were convinced that there was a ghost in the bathroom who did not like them using the toilet.'

As the days passed, and they stayed longer and longer under the night sky, darker stories were told too.

Noni Appa telling him about the night she had gone with Farhan to a friend's party and had overheard a cutting remark by the host about them and Muslims in general. She had been horrified and had tried to get Farhan to leave the party. But he had insisted on staying, nonchalantly walking towards another couple and striking up a conversation.

'I called the waiter, Anand ji, and I gulped two drinks down in less than a minute. Then I went out, found our driver and went home without Farhan. He came after an hour, always had a bit of a temper, you know, and he started yelling, "What do you think of yourself, leaving just like that!" And for the first time I yelled back, "What do you think of yourself, who are you to talk to me like this?"

'He was stunned for a moment and then he said gruffly, "What is wrong with you, Noni?" And I told him, "I am drunk, Farhan, and today I will say whatever I want." Bas, he became like a television on mute, his mouth kept opening and closing but no words came out.' She laughed recalling the incident, now that time and death had smoothened out all the disorderly creases in her marriage.

Anand ji did not talk about his wife except for the time he told Noni Appa about having a close brush with the law. Jyotsna, his wife, in a fit of anger had thrown a big steel utensil at him, it had missed and gone out of the window, crashing down, and had fallen right beside a toddler playing in the compound below.

The building chairman Dr Aggarwal had filed a complaint after calling Anand ji to his house and saying, 'Mr Anand, this was not the first object to go flying out from the windows of flat no. 501. There are many UFOs that have previously taken off from the fifth floor of Clifton. This time I have to take serious action.'

Anand ji had gone to the police station and luckily the case had been dismissed. 'But that was long ago. Over the years she has also changed, from a volcano she has become a pressure cooker. She still has a temper but instead of erupting she just makes a few shrill sounds and lets off steam.'

~

It was Anand ji's birthday in April. 'Which other day can it be on, has to be on April Fool's Day,' Binni teased her sister, when Noni Appa suggested cutting a cake for Anand ji that evening.

Ignoring her sister's cackle, Noni Appa set out to make the day as special as she could for Anand ji. She bought a cake from Monginis bakery, a few balloons and some streamers. She got him a small gift as well, carefully wrapping six audiocassettes together, hits of Mohammed Rafi and Mukesh, his favourite singers.

Having made all the arrangements, she took off for Glory beauty salon to get her hair set. On this occasion, though, she removed the rollers in the parlour itself.

Anand ji was surprised to see a beaming Noni and Binni all dressed up and waiting for him on the porch. They led him to the dining room festooned with the balloons and streamers, and with great enthusiasm sang 'Happy Birthday Anand ji', with Bhondu and Tito also joining the celebrations.

Later that evening, Binni started watching a programme on Doordarshan and Noni Appa and Anand ji went out into the garden to sit in their favourite spot under the trees.

Noni Appa, tilting her face towards the starlit night, pointed out Orion's belt and Orion's two brightest stars, Rigel and Betelgeuse, twinkling on both ends of the constellation.

Anand ji was looking at Noni Appa more than at the sky, thinking about the little celebration she had put together for him. He felt a warm feeling come over him, starting from his chest and spreading outward, though he had not yet sipped from the glass of whisky in his hand.

'I didn't know you liked stargazing,' he said.

Noni Appa, absent-mindedly twisting her hair into a bun and tucking one loose end behind her ear, nodded. 'Yes, because of Abba, when we were little, he would tell Binni and me all about stars, planets and galaxies. See that star there? The light from that star has travelled eight hundred years to reach my eyes. Gazing at it is the smallest way I can pay tribute to its long journey.'

Anand ji gazed at the woman across the table, a tenderness in his eyes that belied the casual way he sat leaning back in his chair. When Noni Appa caught him looking at her, she gave him a shy, embarrassed smile with an almost imperceptible shrug of her tiny shoulders.

One balmy May evening, Anand ji suggested they go for a walk on the beach outside Sea Breeze. Anand ji who had no intention of carrying on the charade that Noni Appa was just his student, despite her insistence, had stopped accepting fees from her for several months. Their relationship though was still undefined and unacknowledged.

When they reached the soft sand near the edge of the sea, Noni Appa removed her slippers and walked barefoot along the shore, slowly, her hip feeling stiff as they walked on in companionable silence. Anand ji cleared his throat and rather tunelessly started singing a popular song, 'Main pal do pal ka shayar hoon', switching from song to song till Noni Appa laughed, 'Are you going to go through the entire weekly countdown of Binaca Geetmala?'

She felt a sharp flare of pain in her hip and they sat down on the sloping sand dune, blending into the landscape with half a dozen couples also on the beach, some with toddlers running towards the sea and the mothers chasing after them.

They were sitting quietly, listening to the sound of the waves and the laughter of the children playing in the sand, when Anand ji, who had stopped calling her Mrs Machiwala as they had got closer, but had found no substitute, finally asked, 'What does Noni mean, is it an Urdu word?'

Noni Appa smiled. 'No, it is just a name our parents used to call us when we were little, Noni and Binni, and it stuck. My real name is Noureen, but just call me Noni Appa like everyone else.'

Anand ji turned towards her, a hint of hesitation in his manner, till he said at last, 'Appa means elder sister, Noni. You are a few years older than me but you are not my sister.' Stumbling over his words, he said, 'There is something I have wanted to tell you for a while. I don't know how to say it and don't even know if I should, because I am a married man but I…' He paused for a moment, afraid and uncertain. Then gathering courage, he continued, 'At our age I can't say that my heart flutters when I am near you, but it hums contentedly, and I want to spend the time I have left listening to that sound.'

Noni Appa straightened the damp blue salwar sticking to her feet. She looked down at her misshapen toes, arthritis having tugged at them till they had finally bent to its will, and said, 'The time to follow our heart has long gone by, Anand ji, the only thing left for the poor thing to do now is to slowly stop.'

She gingerly stood up and they silently walked back together.

The next day Noni Appa spent the afternoon at Muskan, sitting on a chair facing the children who had gathered around her. She was reading aloud from 'The Brahmin and the Three Thugs', intermittently picking up little cut-outs of the characters glued to a stick. But today, unlike her previous read-aloud sessions, she was merely going through the motions.

She found herself thinking about Anand ji, getting annoyed with him, with his need to voice what had simply been understood. Why do people have to define relationships, underline each word till the paper gives way beneath, she wondered.

Anand ji's words had opened a door, spilling light on what Noni Appa had been hiding from everyone including herself. So she had, she hoped, firmly slammed that door shut, because giving up the pretence that this was a mere platonic friendship would mean giving up the relationship as well.

She was a dignified widow, a woman who had led an exemplary life. There was a certain respect in the way people said 'Salaam, Noni Appa' when she walked down the street.

She did not want the same people to start whispering about her, laughing at her, an old woman in an unsavoury affair with a married man. Is this really how she wanted to be remembered? A life spent meticulously polishing and maintaining a gleaming reputation, only to let it tarnish at the very end?

She just hoped that Anand ji would now have the sense to leave things the way they were and that he would not bring up this matter again.

Noni Appa lifted the cut-out of the goat, reading the next four lines, till she stopped abruptly, a sharp-edged pain in her abdomen like a burning knife slicing through. She bent over, dropping the cut-out – and suddenly the pain was gone just as quickly as it had appeared.

Aarti, another volunteer, got her a glass of water and Noni Appa gulped it down gratefully, wiping her clammy forehead with her cotton handkerchief. A little disoriented, she answered Aarti's queries with, 'Like Binni, I think I also can't digest sprouts any more,' referring to the moong salad she'd had for lunch earlier.

Though Noni Appa and Anand ji did not exchange another word about fluttering or humming hearts and went back to their regular ways, the following week brought a perilous predicament right to their gates.

They were wrapping up their card game relatively early on Thursday evening – Noni Appa had been feeling uneasy, the sandwiches lying untouched on the glass table. 'My stomach has just not been all right these days, I am feeling nauseous, Anand ji, I think I will go in and lie down,' she said and was getting up when an autorickshaw stopped outside the gate and she saw Baburam and a plump woman in a printed sari arguing loudly, their words unclear as they melted into the sounds of the busy lane.

Anand ji, who had his back to the gate, turned around as well on hearing the noise. He immediately stood up in surprise. Seeing him, the woman bellowed, 'There he is, I told you my husband is inside. Let me go, you harami, or I will hit you with my slipper!'

She pushed aside a confused Baburam, walked up to Anand ji and, before Noni Appa realized what was happening, swung her bulky arm and slapped the yoga teacher right across the face.

She then turned towards Noni Appa and, giving her a quick, decisive glance, sneered, 'This buddhi is your seven o'clock group class in Bandra?

You kept saying, na, "Jyotsna, it is difficult to get a rickshaw from Pali Hill, takes twenty minutes even if I take the garage road."

'Sala harami, at your age having a chakkar with another woman!' She turned to Noni Appa, adding, 'And you, old hag. Have some shame. If you are so desperate to clean the cobwebs between your legs then go stand on the road outside and look for a man, leave my husband alone!'

And continuing her yelling and screeching till Binni, Bhondu and Tito rushed out into the garden, she dragged a stunned and silent Anand ji to the gate, hailing an autorickshaw swiftly and roughly pushing her husband inside.

~

The din in Anand ji's house reached deafening proportions that Thursday evening and showed no signs of abating. Once again, picture frames were smashed, vases sent flying and mortars and pestles were turned into masala-encrusted missiles.

So many objects seemed to be flying through the air in flat 501 and landing on its tiled floor that one would have thought it was in fact the domestic airport rather than the residence of Anand and Jyotsna Joshi. Even the dogs, Gulab and Jamun – that Anand ji had reluctantly agreed to buy in a moment of absolute cowardice instead of firmly standing up to his wife – crouched behind the sofa, ducking the attacks and adding their sharp barks to their mistress's screeches.

Anand ji, who had at first in guilt-ridden angst been silent, was now, as Sunday afternoon drew to a close, slowly getting enraged at the lifelong bullying he had faced at his wife's hands.

He had never even held Noni's hand and over the last few days he had had to hear all sorts of things. Jyotsna had ranted, 'All you men are like dogs, anyone gives you a biscuit, you wag your tail and lick their hand, but here, God knows what all you must have licked of that dirty old woman.'

Anand ji had tried to protest and Jyotsna had added yet another analogy about dogs. 'What is the difference between you and Gulab?' she yelled, waving towards the tiny, hairy dog. 'He also tries his luck anywhere he can, on Jamun, the sofa leg, the laundry basket, that elephant statue in the corner, anything will do. Just like you trying your luck with that Muslim hag.' She continued, 'I am warning you, if you ever go near that dirty woman again, I will leave this house and never come back.'

Anand ji looked at Jyotsna, her hair dishevelled, face contorted with anger. Age, instead of giving her the happy wrinkles of a life lived with smiles and laughter, had given her the furrowed brow and two deep, vertical lines between her eyebrows that she had truly earned.

He could still see the remnants of the pretty twenty-two-year-old girl he had married. It had seemed like such a splendid match then, with their religion, caste, economic backgrounds completely in sync. Even their horoscopes had been perfectly matched, but living together had soon shown them the vast differences between them.

The many years of anger and hurt now formed a mountain of indignant self-righteousness and regret within him. A man can hear as much music as he pleases in his head but you can only accuse him of disturbing the peace if he plays the record out loud, he told himself. He may have feelings for

Noni but there had been nothing between them. He was ready to stand his ground.

Anand ji had spent the last few decades keeping his head down and waiting for each storm in their marriage to pass. A task that had been easier when he had been busy all day at the BMC office and had his son, Sailesh, as a buffer in the evenings. And though their son would not admit it, Anand ji knew that even Sailesh had fled their volatile home as soon as he could, citing reasons like 'Better prospects in Bangalore, Papa'.

He glanced now at the wreckage of their small living room. It seemed to him that it stood for the wreckage of his life. The first time she had started throwing her weight around, he should have refused to tolerate her temper tantrums, taken a firm stance. Perhaps they would never have reached this point.

He contemplated the years he had left and was filled with dread at the prospect of sitting in his room with his Walkman and headphones, playing solitaire, day after day, till he eventually ran out of days.

He turned to his wife and, with a finality in

his voice that she had never heard before, said, 'Jyotsna, you are welcome to stay and you are welcome to go. You have always done as you pleased and now finally so shall I.'

Leaving her dumbfounded, Anand ji went to his room and firmly locked the door.

Wanting to call her husband's bluff, as she perceived it, Jyotsna threw a few things into a small bag and, screeching through the locked door that he would come crawling to her in a few days, left that very evening.

~

The next afternoon at exactly four-thirty as usual, Anand ji reached Sea Breeze. He decided that he would talk to Noni today, and while playing rummy put all his cards on the table both literally and figuratively.

He pushed the small gate open – Baburam was nowhere in sight – and walked towards the garden, expecting to see Noni sitting on the wrought iron chair. He was surprised to see the lawn deserted. He walked towards the house, calling out to

Bhondu, who came out of the kitchen and said, 'Arrey Anand ji, Memsaab is with Noni Appa in the hospital. Appa started vomiting continuously, she was shivering even after we covered her with many blankets. It has been three days now.'

Anand ji felt a chill in his heart. He hurriedly inquired about the hospital and Bhondu said that Binni had taken Noni Appa to a hospital in Parle.

Nanavati Hospital was a large, white building with a creaky elevator and rickety wooden stairs. The receptionist directed Anand ji to the first floor after sternly informing him that visiting hours were only till 6 p.m.

He climbed up the stairs and entered the waiting area. He spotted Binni and her friend Shamim sitting on the metal chairs. Binni looked pale and distraught, as if she hadn't slept or eaten in days. She had a white muslin dupatta around her head and her fingers were restlessly counting the beads in her tasbih.

When Anand ji asked about Noni, she clutched his hand and said with a tremble, 'Anand ji, it all happened so suddenly. The doctors are saying she had some obstruction in her intestine and has now developed peri…prito something…' and she began weeping, unable to continue. Shamim then added, 'Peritonitis, they are saying her intestine ruptured and she developed peritonitis.'

Anand ji asked, 'How is she now?' And Binni sobbed, 'She is in the ICU. They did the surgery but everything had already become septic inside. Dr Shah was just here. He was saying that she is not responding to antibiotics, her pulse is falling, blood urea and creatinine are very high. Her kidneys are shutting down. Allah can't be so cruel to take her from me, Anand ji. She is all that I have left.'

Anand ji sat down on the metal chair, feeling drained all of a sudden, an overwhelming fatigue creeping over him.

When visiting hours ended, Anand ji advised Binni to go home and rest. He would stay the night and promised to call her as soon as he got any information.

He sat on the metal chair alongside numerous other people who also had their loved ones in the ICU. Some slept with their bags serving as pillows, some prayed and some just sat looking fixedly at the swinging doors of the ICU wing in apprehension.

Early dawn brought a flutter of activity in the waiting room with a middle-aged woman wailing inconsolably when she was informed that her father had passed away. Anand ji rubbed his eyes, rotated his stiff neck and walked up to the nurse's station to ask about Noni's condition.

A bespectacled nurse replied, 'It's same only. Doctor coming out, you ask to him.'

When Dr Shah came out of the ICU he informed Anand ji that Noni Appa's condition remained critical. They had started her on a new antibiotic but if that did not work she would soon go into multiple organ failure. Anand ji went into the ICU to see Noni.

He saw her lying on the bed, hooked to an IV pole, a tube in one nostril to suck out fluid from her stomach and electrodes attached to her chest leading to a heart monitor. He reached out and touched her cheek gently. Though he had imagined this moment dozens of times, not once had he thought it would be at a time like this.

Binni came to the hospital a few hours later

and Anand ji went home to freshen up. He made himself a cup of tea and though he opened a packet of biscuits he found himself unable to eat any. He lay down on the bed, closing his eyes, hoping to sleep for an hour but he kept seeing a lifeless Noni lying on the hospital bed. Restless, he returned to the hospital.

Binni met him in the waiting room. She seemed ebullient. 'Anand ji, good news, Noni Appa is conscious. You know, I had not told Mallika till now, but I will make a call in the evening and tell her. These rubbish doctors had said that Noni Appa had nearly departed, but my Noni is too strong and with Allah's blessings she has now made a U-turn.'

Noni Appa was in the hospital for fifteen days and Anand ji spent all his time with her once she was moved out of the ICU to a regular room. He sat next to her, holding her hand, reading aloud to her from a Hindi novel with a lurid cover that Binni had brought along.

After she complained about the smell of hospitals, the stomach-turning odour of vomit and disinfectant, he brought her a new string of sweet-smelling jasmine flowers to keep near her pillow every day.

When Noni Appa left the hospital, it was he who accompanied her to her flat. He picked up Noni Appa's small suitcase, took the key from her, unlocked the door and entered the small house that belonged to the long-departed Farhan and the nearly departed Noni.

Anand ji visited her every evening, sitting in the balcony with her, drinking a cup of tea while making sure she drank enough juice and milk as it would be weeks before she could consume solids again. As Binni bustled about in Noni Appa's small flat, gossiping loudly about the latest scandals, Anand ji would sit by her side, propping a pillow behind her back, playing rummy with her.

Noni Appa, who all these years had lived solely by the dictates of society, began realizing that all the 'Salaams' and 'Ya Ali Madads' that people bestowed on her as a reward for being a respectable woman were worthless, a currency that would buy her nothing aside from synthetic eulogies at her funeral.

After her hospital stay and her brief tussle with

the djinns of death, she had slowly come to the conclusion that the only people truly there for her were Binni and Anand ji. So how did it matter what the world deemed correct or incorrect?

She had to loosen these strings that tied her down because time was untying the knots with such great speed at the other end and pulling her lower and lower to the ground each day, till soon she would be buried underneath.

This time it was Noni who brought up matters of the heart. One evening, sitting in the balcony, she said, 'Do you remember what you said that day on the beach, Anand ji? I was so foolish that I refused to hear you out, foolish that I have spent most of my life worrying about what people will say, how they will perceive me.

'Anand ji, I can see the finishing line in the mist ahead and I too want to reach the end listening to my heart hum.' And she held his arm, resting her head against his shoulder.

Soon Anand ji moved his meagre belongings into Noni Appa's spare room. She had got it repainted from a dull cream to an eggshell blue for him, erasing sticker marks and scratches from the posters and picture frames that Mallika had once hung on the walls.

Anand ji had left Jyotsna the apartment in Clifton and the rental from a small flat they had in Mahim. Jyotsna had tried to make things difficult by involving various relatives and friends to intervene and even intimidate Anand ji into returning to Clifton.

But Anand ji had stood his ground. He had finally asked Sailesh to come down from Bangalore and talk to his mother. Sailesh, having grown up witnessing the brittle relationship between his parents, had explained to his mother the futility of continuing to live a life filled with conflict. In this final stretch of their lives, he argued, it would be good for both of them to find peace and happiness. Jyotsna then retreated into a stony silence.

Noni Appa, on her part, had written Mallika a letter outlining her plans. Mallika called her mother promptly from London exclaiming, 'What a sly fox you are, Mom!' And then captivated by the prospect that life doesn't really end at sixty, as she had lately begun to fear, she asked, 'Mom, so is Anand ji the great love of your life then? The one you have been waiting for, to sweep you off your feet?'

Noni Appa laughed. 'Don't be silly! Sweeping me off my feet – only your father could do that. We are perfectly happy but it's not my-heart-beating-fast kind of love. If it were, then at this age I would have a heart attack, wouldn't I? But it's wonderful to have a companion.'

And while talking to her daughter about Anand ji, Noni Appa realized that in their own way they had in fact found love, like a well-worn cashmere sweater that hugs in the right places and doesn't tug at the wrong ones while keeping you warm on wintry days.

~

Noni Appa brought two cups of tea and placed them on the small wooden table next to Anand ji. It had taken a year but she had finally made a full recovery though she had still not dared to have her favourite Scotch on the rocks.

She sat on the rattan chair opposite Anand ji. Waving towards the cloudy blue sky, he said, 'It has not rained the whole day today, Noni, have you noticed? You know, it is said that during Tansen's time he could light a fire by singing Raga Deepak and if you wanted it to rain all you had to do was sing Raga Megh Malhar.'

And just like that Anand ji began singing 'Meghshyam Ghanashyam' in Raga Megh Malhar, 'Yeeeeaa aaa yeeeeeee ji...'

Noni Appa calmly switched off her hearing aid and continued sipping her tea slowly. An hour later, the clouds darkened to a dusty grey and it started drizzling.

Anand ji looked at her with childlike glee – though it couldn't quite be considered a miracle since it was July and Bombay was in the middle of the monsoon season. But she, patting him on his shoulder, smiled all the same, as they sat together in silence, watching the rain fall, in the manner of a leaky faucet, all drips and drops, on the branches of the gulmohar tree.

If the Weather Permits

The weather forecast in the *Indian Express* had predicted a week of sunshine but on the day that Elisa Thomas was getting married for the third time to the same man, it began to rain.

It had been a cloudless day during the simple civil ceremony at the courthouse in Bandra three days ago. Overcast yesterday, when Elisa had become Ayesha, converting to her husband's religion. The ceremony had lasted all of twenty minutes and the good Christian girl forgot her new name as soon as she removed the mint green kurta and billowing silk sharara pants with their intricate gold zardozi work embroidered in a little dusty workshop in faraway Lucknow.

Today, at her third wedding at St Thomas Marthoma Syrian Church, the pouring rain obscuring the stained-glass windows made the interiors look dreary and grey.

Elisa Thomas tried to look calm as she stood still in front of the slightly damp and disgruntled priest but all she could think about, as she glanced nervously towards the windows, was the garden party after and whether the rains would cut short the celebrations.

She cut an imposing figure, three inches taller than the groom, her long, brown hair pulled tightly away from her coffee-coloured face in a severe bun, her perpetually arched eyebrows looming over her small, thickly lashed eyes. Today she was clad in a delicate white sari with a red silk one draped over her head that she would change into for the wedding reception.

Her husband, Javed Gazi, a professional photographer, who at thirty-seven still nursed dreams of joining the Indian cricket team as a fast bowler, wore a borrowed black suit and a stoic grimace.

Elisa's father, Pothen Thomas, or Acha as she called him, sat in the first pew holding on to his Christianity like he was the weary custodian of the last crumbling communion wafer. He had lost one battle when his eldest daughter, Rahel, married a Punjabi banker. And though the chances of Elisa giving him three or four curly-haired grandchildren with names like Ninan and Cherian had always been rather unlikely, having to finally face this grim reality filled him with bleakness.

He turned to his wife, Jincy, a string of orange kanakambaram flowers in her hair, a maroon silk sari tightly wrapped around her overweight frame, dozens of gold rings gleaming on her fingers, and whispered, 'All the nice Malayali IPS officers we kept inviting over for tea and Marie biscuits, she rejected. And then she had to go and marry this Javed!'

Pothen Thomas's eyes misted up behind his thick black bifocals as he continued, 'You tell me, in this India of so many billion peoples, she could not find a boy, okay not Christian or Malayali but at least an Indian boy? Had to find this Muslim refugee from third-rate country Bangladesh!'

Jincy, without moving her eyes from her daughter and her new son-in-law, maintained a tight-lipped smile on her heavily powdered face and whispered, 'Pothen, mark my words, it will not last even six months!'

Jincy Thomas was wrong – it lasted for nine.

~

Room no. 10 at the Hotel du Globe et des Quatre-Vents was decorated with an antique bed, a silk bedspread and fresh yellow flowers. The only drawback was that it was so tiny that they had to squeeze past each other to go to the bathroom.

Elisa would usually open the room door and stand outside, in the hotel corridor, till she heard the sound of the toilet flushing, waiting till her husband made the trek back towards the other side of the room. But these inconveniences did not matter because she was in Paris.

Every morning, Javed and Elisa would open maps and notebooks at the pastry shop next door, and over cups of steaming black coffee and buttery croissants they would plan their separate itineraries for the day.

Though it was odd that two people on their honeymoon would choose to spend the entire day apart, Javed only wanted to go to the art galleries and museums, while Elisa wanted to see all the tourist attractions like the Arc de Triomphe and the Eiffel Tower. So they would go off on their independent adventures and meet each other in time for dinner.

There was yet another odd thing about this honeymoon: there was no sex. No wooden headboard banging against the wall; no long brown legs, covered in sweat, being pried apart; no moans filtering through the wafer-thin wallpapered partitions and spilling into room no. 9, disturbing the elderly German couple that Elisa saw sometimes in the corridor.

Javed and Elisa had been dating for eight years, an on-off-on-off relationship like a defective light fixture. As time went by, they began sleeping with friends and sometimes strangers during their off periods, but during their on periods, gradually without quite knowing why, they stopped having sex with each other.

This desolate area of their relationship did not bother Elisa. She had married Javed partly because she had a bond with him and also because she needed to get married before she would inevitably, one weary day, succumb to one of the Malayali boys, a Varghese or a Joseph, it didn't matter which, that her parents used as battering rams to break her defences down.

Walking down to Pont de l'Alma in the 8th Arrondissement to catch a ferry and see the Notre Dame against the slanting evening sunlight, she felt that this life with Javed was good enough.

Elisa had been on another ferry ride, not so long ago, crossing over from Versova to Madh Island with her older sister Rahel and Luke, her little nephew, holding a picnic basket. Rahel leaned against the rusty iron railing, the salt air turning her blow-dried hair into a frizzy mess, and asked her, 'Elisa, why are you like this? Don't you think you should stop slipping in and out of relationships and find the right man?'

Taking a sip from a bottle of Kingfisher beer, Elisa replied, 'You know, this reminds me of something a man told me just yesterday, "Things have a way of turning up when they want to be found, though they may not always be the things you actually want to find."'

Rahel, squinting in the sun, said, 'That's pretty profound, Eli, he's a spiritual guru or something?'

And Elisa, the corners of her eyes crinkling up, laughed. 'No! He was just stoned, Rahel!'

Javed was perhaps the right man, Elisa thought as she took pictures of the Jardin Tino Rossi, wandering through the sculpture garden and surrounding lawns on her way back to the hotel. He needed a lot of space, which meant that she, in return, got the space to do what she wanted as well. There were no restrictions on her, no demands.

And she liked listening to him talk about art and books. Javed had lithographs, and a charcoal sketch by Souza next to his study table. There was a dusty bookshelf in one corner of his bedroom, with slim red volumes filled with poems by Rumi, Roald Dahl's *Dirty Beasts*, a battered book of Ghalib's poetry. These were not things she had grown up with in her two-bedroom house that always smelled of meen moilee, a watery fish curry that her mother insisted on making five times a week.

Eight days in Paris and they were back in Bombay, enclosed in Javed's small flat at Yari Road. Elisa went back to working at her father's real estate firm while Javed spent his days earning his living as a photographer. In the evenings, he would practise his bowling, which inevitably led to a sprained shoulder or an aching back, while she would go off visiting friends or occasionally paint, leaving a series of unfinished canvases stacked in their garage below.

Javed was a quiet man who, aside from a beer or two on rare occasions, did not like drinking; nor did he smoke or socialize. His only weakness was that he visited numerous psychiatrists, palmists, fortune tellers and faith healers, trying to find anything that might dispel the dark fog that often filled his mind.

It was Elisa who was the gregarious one, with hordes of friends and a bad smoking habit. She would often go dancing till dawn and when she returned, her hair full of smoke, her mouth tasting of wine, and tumbled into bed, he would move over, and turn his back to her, pretending to be asleep.

With time, Javed got quieter and Elisa was out more often. The shadowy nebula of resentment in Javed's mind seemed to get bigger and bigger till

Elisa could feel it when she brushed against him. It would encircle her when she passed him a cup of tea, sit between them during dinner, lie beside them in bed – like an invisible third person in their marriage.

This silent stalemate could have continued indefinitely but it didn't. That December they travelled to Goa with Elisa's friends to celebrate New Year's Eve. Javed, riding a motorbike with Elisa holding on to him, poured half a bottle of Old Port rum down his throat. He told Elisa that he wanted to die and rammed their bike into a passing truck.

Elisa wrenched the handlebars from him, so they ended up falling in a ditch on the side of the road instead. Javed broke his nose, a rib and his right shoulder. Elisa had a scratch on her arm, straw in her hair and dirt stains on her sparkly silver top.

She returned to the hotel, called her sister and said, 'Rahel, since it's New Year's Eve it's better to start the next year on a good note. You will tell Achan to do the paperwork for me, right?' And she returned home to live with her Achan and her Amma, in the house that always smelled of meen moilee.

~

Two years went by where Elisa went from one relationship to the next like she was trying on a pair of jeans, slipping it on, twirling around and then leaving it in a crumpled heap on the floor.

She eventually found one that came close to her idea of perfection – a Rajasthani man called Ajay Shekhawat. But his family, inclined towards politics, had already arranged his marriage to a girl that could strengthen their political clout. Afraid that Elisa would end up with a bullet in her head, Jincy decided to take matters into her own hands. She bought the thirty-one-year-old Elisa a conservative salwar kameez and took her to Trivandrum.

Chacko was the son of the local district collector Abraham Kurien, and at forty he had never been married. He was tall, had the ubiquitous moustache that all South Indian men sport as a sign of virility, a receding hairline and was wearing a Black Sabbath T-shirt with blue jeans. He sat next to his father quietly watching Elisa.

Jincy began, 'Elisa, you know Chacko's uncle is a bishop and his grandfather was also a bishop. Such distinguished people in your family, Mr Kurien.'

Over a meal of appams and some chakkakuru manga curry made with jackfruit seeds, coconut and mango, Elisa discovered that Mr Kurien was an engaging man.

They sighed about the dwindling Jewish community in Kerala, the handful of Malabari Jews and even fewer Paradesi Jews that were now left, making the Paradesi the smallest Jewish community in the world. Mr Kurien regaled them with a ghost story about the Lakkidi gateway haunted by a tribal leader called Karinthandan who during the Raj helped a British engineer find the shortest route to Thamarassery and was murdered.

Elisa thought she could live in this large, rambling house with Mr Kurien and his son, on old-time stories and funny anecdotes. At least here she wouldn't have to continually bump into her parents and their reproachful faces. But first she needed to exchange a few words with her prospective husband who had barely opened his mouth.

'So, Chacko,' said Elisa, after Mr Kurien led them to the first-floor study, 'what do you do?'

Chacko pulled out a joint from the pocket of his jeans and asked her, 'You smoke ganja?' When she nodded tentatively, he lit the joint and offered it to Elisa. After she had a long drag, he said, 'I studied management, we bought a seat in some college in America, but I didn't finish. I watch television and drink beer.'

Though most women would have jumped out of their chair, screeching, 'Amma, save me!' Elisa who had always looked at her life as if it were an episode of *Star Trek* – adhering faithfully to its slogan 'To boldly go where no man has gone before' – immediately decided to explore this uncharted, idle planet to a resounding round of applause by her elated parents. It wouldn't be just an adventure, she thought to herself, but she'd actually please her parents for the first time in her adult life.

~

The weather forecast in Kerala's leading newspaper, *Deepika*, stated that it would be a week filled with clear skies and, unlike the much more widely circulated *Indian Express*, it was accurate on both the days Elisa got married.

For the civil ceremony she had picked a white-and-red dress with daffodils and for the church wedding she wore the same delicate white sari she had for her last wedding as she felt it would be a waste to buy yet another one.

Elisa stood in front of Father James Chandy at St Rita's Malankara Church in Trivandrum with Chacko. Her entire family had gathered to watch her getting married for the fifth time except her sister, Rahel, who refused to fly down saying, 'Elisa, if you just want the excitement of jumping without quite knowing where you are going to land, try skydiving. But I am not interested in witnessing this holding the nose, ignoring the stinky water and taking a dip, just to see how it makes you feel. If I were you, I would tell Amma and Achan to call off this farce.'

Elisa lashed out at her sister, 'And do what? Watch Achan watch me every day, wondering what he's supposed to do with me now, when he can pass this ticking time bomb on to some other unsuspecting Malayali victim? No thanks!'

Two days later, Elisa and Chacko left for their honeymoon in a white Maruti Gypsy with a boot filled with snacks and beer. They were going to take turns and drive along a scenic route that took them from Trivandrum all the way to Cochin.

Elisa drove for the first hour, Chacko looking out of the window, smoking a joint and passing it to Elisa intermittently. When they switched places, Elisa grabbed a beer and, despite the heavy metal music playing on the car stereo, soon fell asleep.

Elisa was dreaming, she was in a garden, in the coils of a labyrinth, the green hedge high above her head. She was leaving a trail of teeth behind her as she walked on. There was a cat somewhere though she could not see it.

The cat kept mewling and whimpering, her cries ringing in her ears. Elisa frowned, she was half awake now. Her eyes shut but she could still hear the cat. She opened her eyes. The music was off and Chacko, tears rolling down his cheeks, was bawling that he wanted to kill himself.

Elisa's first thought was, 'Crap! What are the chances of this happening all over again!' Followed by, 'I need to take control of this vehicle before this crazy bugger rams it somewhere.' Elisa leaned over, swerved the steering wheel towards the side of the road and made Chacko stop the car.

She tried talking to Chacko but he had withdrawn into silence. He kept snivelling and refused to speak. She wondered what to do, contemplated heading back but decided that it was a nice road trip to Brunton Boatyard in Cochin. She might as well see it all now. Everything was booked and God knows when she would get the chance again.

Hundred and sixty kilometres later they reached Alleppey. Elisa parked the car, picked up their bags and, followed by a silent Chacko, checked into the houseboat. She lay down on the bed, looking at the sprawling backwaters from the wooden window as the houseboat cruised along the narrow canals with paddy fields and coconut groves along the sides. Chacko sat outside, near the prow of the houseboat, his eyes shut, head drooping to one side, chewing on a piece of stale gum.

She ate rice with spicy prawn curry that burned the back of her throat and made her nose drip but a silent Chacko refused to eat anything at all. His was not an aggressive silence. He would smile, nod, and sit by the carrom board in the room fiddling with the wooden playing discs. It seemed to be a congenial stupor.

The next morning they drove for a couple of hours to stay at a cardamom plantation in Thekkady. Chacko seemed better. He even drove for an hour or so and they talked – about the best route to take, the weather, an old aunt who believed in voodoo. Elisa decided to leave yesterday where she felt it belonged, a hundred kilometres behind her.

The new bride consummated her marriage that night, reluctantly. Chacko reached out to her in the dark. Though she tried telling him that it wasn't the right time, making excuses about menstruating, Chacko went ahead.

Later, lying in the creaky, warm bed, she wondered if he had even noticed the spotless white bed sheet that showed up her white lie but Chacko was snoring, sleeping in a fetal position, facing away from her.

Elisa tried comforting herself with the fact that though the sex had been just about adequate, with a little tutoring it had the potential to become pretty darn good.

But lying in a strange bed with an even stranger man, the brazen carefreeness that she usually armed herself with failed her.

In the darkness, she sensed the empty space that lurked inside her, which she kept away with laughter and company; the vast loneliness that had brought her to this point, where she was now married to a man whom she not only hardly knew but had no interest in knowing better. Elisa spent half the night staring at the ceiling fan as it turned round and round endlessly, moving continuously but not going anywhere.

The drive to Brunton Boatyard was a long one

and around midday Chacko started muttering about meeting angels. This was interspersed with smiles and comments like 'It's better not to wake up a hungry man than not to give him food.' And 'Nice line depth!'

Luckily he fell asleep, only to wake up just as they were pulling into the driveway of Brunton Boatyard. He opened the door of the moving car and rushed inside, babbling feverishly, 'My angel is waiting for me!'

Elisa sat in the car debating whether to simply turn the car around and drive all the way back to Trivandrum, pack her bags and fly back to Bombay. Her reverie was broken when a security guard and what seemed to be two men from the hotel management frantically requested her to come inside.

She saw Chacko in the lobby, trying to grab a gym bag that was dangling from the shoulder of an overweight, red-faced Russian man while hollering, 'I have found my angel! Come with me!'

Elisa managed to calm Chacko down and bundle him into their room. Back in the lobby, the Russian asked her, 'Are you the wife? What is the problem with him?' As she tried to apologize to him, Elisa explained, 'I don't know anything about him. You see, we have only been married for five days.'

A few days later Elisa was back at the house that always smelled of meen moilee. Pothen Thomas opened the door, looked at his daughter, then looked at the three suitcases next to her and called out to his wife, 'Jincy, come here! Again she has come back home!' So Elisa decided to go and live with Rahel instead.

~

Elisa was sitting at her desk at the office when she saw Chacko walking in with her father. It had been two months since she had last seen him. Chacko gave Elisa one of his vacant smiles as he sat in the reception area, while Pothen pulled his disgruntled daughter into his cabin.

Elisa said, 'Acha, did you ask him to come here? I don't want to have anything to do with him. He is totally mad, you know!' Pothen Thomas was livid. 'Always everyone is mad, Elisa, everyone but you! A woman who does not have a man's name behind her is the mad one. People will trouble her non-stop. Deaf and dumb but a man is a man is a man.'

So Elisa was made to leave Rahel's house and move back into the house with Achan, Amma and their house guests, Chacko and Mr Kurien.

If Elisa's parents noticed anything strange about Chacko's penchant for suddenly saying things like 'There is a lock on my icebox!' or staring silently at a dot on the wall for hours on end, they did not comment.

One evening, over a dinner of – what else? – meen moilee, potatoes, dosas and steamed rice, Mr Kurien said, 'Elisa, give Chacko a chance. He has been through a lot. When he was hospitalized the doctor said that he suffers from a minor mental illness like depression but he got better and they released him. He is doing well now. His cousin Joseph Idiculas also had some problems like this, but now he has three children. Elisa, have a child with Chacko and he will become all right, I guarantee it.'

Elisa glanced at Chacko, who was now smiling

softly at the rava dosa on his plate. She looked at Jincy and Pothen, who were nodding agreeably, and said, 'Mr Kurien, if you think having sex will make your son better, then I am happy to arrange dozens of girls for him. But if you tell me to have intercourse with him and have a baby, then I am not volunteering. I have no desire for my gravestone to bear an epitaph stating "Here lies buxom Mother Teresa who sacrificed her life by curing mental disabilities through her vagina."'

And as Pothen Thomas started thinking about all the paperwork he would have to do all over again, Chacko looked up from his plate and in a strange moment of perfect lucidity said, 'Elisa, you have a kind vagina.'

~

A year later, Elisa sat with Rahel, knitting a white woollen blanket for her newborn niece. Rahel, who still looked vaguely pregnant, despite the baby being three months old, sat in the rocking chair putting her baby to sleep.

Pothen Thomas walked briskly into the

room, holding a newspaper, and said, 'Elisa, see this newspaper! It says that Makhija Builders' daughter, she is a Manglik. I know this fellow, I have gone to his office also one or two times. She is having to marry a tree before she is getting married to some diamond merchant chap.

'This article tells that according to astrological texts, Mangliks can never have happy marriage till they perform this tree wedding first, otherwise harm falls on the husband, he goes mental or even dies. Your horoscope also says that you are a Manglik. I don't know why we never thought of this, maybe we should also try. And then after that, get you married to a nice Malayali boy...'

Rahel interrupted her father, 'Acha, you are already talking about getting her remarried when that mad Chacko is refusing to sign the divorce papers!'

Pothen ignored his daughter and continued, 'I know George Mathai is looking for his son. After all, a man is a man is a man.'

Elisa, looking away from her father, her head towards the window, murmured, 'Yes Acha, deaf and dumb, a man is everything, I have heard this before; but the day I want to settle down with a stable, deeply rooted member of the community, I will marry the tree.'

Later that month, Elisa left her Achan and Amma and the house that always smelled of meen moilee for the last time. She told Pothen that she knew she could not change her parents or change her own mindset, so she was going to change the only thing she could, her postal address.

She was going to move to the small house her grandmother had left Rahel and her in their ancestral home town of Oyoor located on the banks of the Ithikkara river.

Rahel had asked her, 'Won't you get lonely there, Eli?' and she replied, 'It will be far less lonely than sharing a name and a bed with yet another stranger. Been there done that, have two marriage certificates, not just the proverbial T-shirt.'

Elisa paused for a moment and then she said, 'Achan and Amma have always been so proud of you, Rahel. "Our daughter is a senior director in the HR department of Microsoft," they go around telling everyone. But I am just a thorn in their side, one that pricks them every day when they see my face; the daughter who can get nothing right including the simple task that even fools seem to manage perfectly well, marriage.

'To tell you the truth, I am looking forward to going, I will paint, read, maybe even open a school for primary students, learn to like myself all over again.'

Looking at her sister getting all teary-eyed, Elisa exclaimed, 'For God's sake, don't start crying now, I am not going away forever, I'll be back for a visit around Christmas.'

Elisa never reached Oyoor. On National Highway 66, close to Kayamkulam, a truck carrying timber overturned and crashed into her small Maruti Suzuki.

~

On a postcard-perfect day with clear blue skies, Elisa Thomas was buried in the presence of her distraught family. Pothen and Jincy had wanted to engrave Elisa's gravestone with 'Elisa Thomas: Beloved daughter, sister and wife.'

But Rahel, half-crazed with grief, had screamed

at her father, 'Elisa would not even have been on that road if it were not for you. Deaf and dumb but a man is a man is a man is not only the most idiotic thing I have ever heard, but it is fucking grammatically fucking incorrect!'

The Christian cemetery at Sewri has a simple white arched gate. Tall, wide-branched trees dapple sunlight over tombstones with marble cherubs and cast their shade over lonely, unmarked graves as well. Far on the left side, next to a bush filled with tiny blue flowers, lies a simple tombstone with an epitaph that says: Here lies Elisa, she briefly belonged to many, but truly to herself.

The Sanitary Man from a Sacred Land

1

On a sweltering afternoon in a small town near Dewas in Madhya Pradesh, Bablu Kewat was carefully cycling on a bumpy road. He took out a checked handkerchief from the breast pocket of his maroon shirt and was about to wipe his sweaty forehead when he spotted two of his childhood friends, Naamdev and Hariprasad, standing under the shade of a banyan tree, chewing tobacco.

Bablu raised his arm and called out to them. They looked at him and instead of returning his greeting began to walk away from him, down the slope towards the paddy field. The smile on Bablu's broad face faded. Looking weary, even his thin moustache seeming to droop in disappointment, he hunched his shoulders and quickly pedalled on.

The dusty road began to narrow. Houses

appeared on either side – bright-coloured structures, some with television antennas popping out of the ubiquitous blue plastic sheets covering holes in their roofs. He had to carefully navigate the bustling street crowded with women in green and orange saris, strings of jasmine flowers wrapped around their buns like soft clouds of scented wonder; little girls in blue uniforms, their pigtails tied with bright red ribbons, walking home after school; and two- and three-wheelers that honked intermittently at stray cows blocking their path.

A sudden spray of tiny pebbles made Bablu's bicycle wobble. He looked around, trying to find the mischief-maker, only to see some schoolboys, pebbles still in hand, looking straight at him and laughing mockingly. He recognized one of the boys as the shopkeeper Ganjkaran's son but decided to ignore them.

A small, freshly painted house loomed ahead, his pride and joy, coated with Asian Paints' White Satin by Bablu himself just a few months ago. He parked his bicycle, unhooked the plastic bag dangling from the handlebar, slung it over his shoulder and with a thick metal chain locked his cycle to the pole outside his house.

As he was walking towards his door, he heard a familiar nasal voice call out, 'Pervert!' He looked up – it was his neighbour's wife Parul, standing at her kitchen window glaring at him, her gold nose pin gleaming in the sun as she washed the dishes.

He stood still, looking back at her. If he could not call her names, he could at least show her that she did not cow him. She, aside from being an expert gossip, was an expert at the art of intimidation and did not back down.

Minutes passed with both refusing to lower their gaze. Bablu began to get bored with this 'waiting without blinking' game, and invented a new one. Keeping his gaze fixed on her, he began to chant dha dhin dhin dha – the simple, repetitive beat that he had learnt playing the tabla as a child – and began fumbling through a series of vigorous dance movements, flinging his arms about, balancing precariously on one leg. It was the most eccentric kind of ballet, a clumsy cross between Kathak and the moves he had seen in Bollywood films.

Parul looked at him puzzled, but when he continued with his ungainly pirouettes and started advancing towards her, she nervously shrieked, 'Gowri, Gowri! Come out!'

Bablu's wife, Gowri, rushed outside, with Choti, their dog, following closely at her heels. Seeing her husband leaping around like a lunatic in the sun, she said, 'Stop this! What are you doing?' He immediately came to an awkward halt, not wanting to tell her what Parul had called him.

It would set off yet another argument between the two of them – and these had been happening too often for his liking. He muttered softly, 'If she is going to stare at me each time I come home, I may as well give her something to look at.'

Parul, sensing that she once again had the upper hand, her prodigious stomach pressing against the windowsill, leaned out of her kitchen window, pointed at Bablu and, in a voice dripping with scorn, said, 'Gowri, why don't you take your husband to some big doctor, he is stark raving mad, I tell you!'

Gowri, her head lowered, silently tugged at

her husband's arm, pulling him towards the open front door.

Bablu hung his shirt and grey pants on a hook behind the door and changed into an airy cotton vest and a pair of worn-out pyjamas. He sat cross-legged on the cement floor waiting for Gowri to place the steel plates filled with their lunch on the floor.

Gowri had not uttered a single word since they had walked inside. Her green glass bangles jingled angrily as she went about her chores, the only sound that broke the stifling silence between the husband and wife.

Bearing a single plate heaped with rice, cauliflower curry and some sliced onions, she placed it with a sharp thud in front of him. Bablu looked at his wife searchingly.

A little more than a year ago Gowri had been a stranger and now here she was, his life partner, the one person who was meant to stand by his side through the good and bad times.

Gowri was a small-built woman with a nondescript face, and deep-set brown eyes under her thick eyebrows. Her most striking feature was a charming smile that revealed a tiny gap between her two front teeth and softened her face to girlishness. It was the smile that he had noticed when they first met at her mother's house. A smile that he had not seen for many weeks now.

Bablu caught her hand and pulled her down to sit beside him. 'Gowri, please stop this, come here.' And when she did not respond, he asked, 'Do you also believe what I am doing is wrong?' Gowri finally looked at him and said, 'It does not matter if it is right or wrong, please just stop all this. Everyone in the town is saying you have lost your mind. You want to know the truth? Even your mother has gone to consult Goraksh Baba hoping he can suggest some remedy!'

Bablu sighed. 'There is no point in explaining anything to you people.' He finished his meal in silence, feeling tired and heavy. And though he desperately wanted to lie down and rest, he decided that this was the best time to finish his work. The roads would all be empty, the intense afternoon heat driving everyone indoors.

Bablu stood up, opened the dented Godrej cupboard in one corner of the room, rummaged under his shirts till he found the sanitary napkin and placed it inside the briefs that he had bought especially for the occasion – it was a snug brown pair, very different from what he usually wore, loose, striped boxers that dangled almost till his knees.

He then took out a rubber bladder filled with blood from the plastic bag he had brought home. He inserted a tube at one end and strapped the contraption to his hip gingerly with duct tape, already anticipating the pain when he would have to rip it off.

The other end of the tube he tucked inside his new briefs. He pulled on his pants and put his maroon shirt back on. Calling out, 'Gowri, I left something unfinished at the workshop; I will be back in an hour or so,' he left the house.

Bablu walked around the neighbourhood, pressing the rubber bladder every now and then and feeling the damp, sticky blood accumulate on the sanitary napkin. Within half an hour there was a noxious odour surrounding him.

To his dismay he discovered that the lower end of the tube had slipped away from the sanitary

113

napkin, out of his underwear, and there was blood all over his crotch. He wanted to rush home immediately before anyone saw him but if Gowri spotted him with bloodstained pants it would lead to a war worse than the Mahabharata. He hurried to a nearby well, hoping to swiftly scrub his pants and then go home.

The well was deserted aside from three stray dogs fighting over a dead mouse and a sickly looking goat lying down near it. He took off his pants, and as he sat scrubbing at the bloodstains, he saw Parul's younger sister Lata walking towards the well.

She looked at Bablu quizzically as she came closer. He tried to stand up and pull his wet pants on, but accidentally pressed the bladder instead and a large squirt of blood sprinkled over the well, the goat and the muddy ground.

Lata stood still for a minute, shocked at this spectacle. Then she started screaming and made a noisy getaway, startling several cows and four half-naked boys who were all defecating on the side of the road one kilometre to the north.

The next day myriad rumours spread all over

the small town. Bablu had turned into a demon, he was a vampire who wanted to suck the blood of virgins, he was involved in perverse sexual activities with female goats. Parul paraded Lata in front of the entire neighbourhood as the lucky victim who all thanks to God's kindness had escaped from Bablu's diabolical intentions.

Gowri, who burst into hysterical tears on hearing about the incident, finally called her brother to fetch her and went to stay at her mother's house for an indefinite period of time.

2

Bablu was not a vampire or a demon and aside from looking on in alarm when he accidentally sprayed blood all over the goat he had no interest in it either, sexual or otherwise. He was a simple welder whose life had been ripped apart all because he had wanted to give Gowri a gift.

Bablu and Gowri had had an arranged marriage, after meeting just once, briefly, in the presence of both their families.

Gowri in a blue-and-gold sari with pink lipstick inexpertly applied over her lips entered the small living room and sat across the tall, thin stranger who was about to be her prospective groom.

Bablu did not quite know what to make of this creature with her head bowed and her eyes lowered, but as he kept looking at her, Gowri's little nephew sitting beside her whispered something in her ear and she smiled, a radiant, toothy grin that lingered in her eyes for a few moments even after she quickly schooled her features.

Kanchan Bua, Gowri's aunt, pointed at the potato-filled kachoris and the jalebis on the table and addressed Bablu's mother, Bhairavi Kewat, 'Bhairavi ji, like I told you Gowri is a wonderful cook, she has made the kachoris, do try one.'

Bablu's mother leisurely sipped her tea and then had a small bite of the piping-hot delicacy. She was examining Gowri as she would a basket of tomatoes in Patri market, like she wanted to pick her up and turn her around, fingers jabbing against the skin, looking for defects.

After a few minutes of silent deliberation over Gowri's possible virtues against her probable imperfections, Bhairavi Kewat finally said, 'Kanchan ji, you were right, the kachoris are indeed marvellous.' And the matter was settled.

A letter was sent shortly afterwards with Bablu's and, more importantly, his mother's consent. And after a small wedding on an auspicious day in March, Gowri became Mrs Prabhash Ram Kewat, Bablu's official name that was never used anywhere except on government documents like his ration card.

3

In the first few months of their life together, Bablu would make it a point to surprise Gowri with small gifts, telling her to close her eyes and then placing little objects in her hand, four bangles, a packet of orange bindis, a 5 Star chocolate. These tiny gifts would be elaborately packed, sometimes in large green leaves, sometimes with the glossy sections of old newspapers.

An arranged marriage is a peculiar situation where you marry a complete stranger and then go about determinedly trying to fall in love with them. It is also crucial in the early stages of this strange experiment that both parties try to put their best foot forward, husbands often by simply refraining from publicly scratching their groins, and wives by trying to please their mothers-in-law, formerly easy-going women who almost instantly turn into eagle-eyed perfectionists with the arrival of a daughter-in-law.

Bablu Ram Kewat's whimsically wrapped gifts were his way of weaving tenderness into a marriage that only had the hardened bricks of shared caste and economic backgrounds as its foundations. His attempts seemed to work – because Gowri always had her childlike smile to offer him as a gift of her own when he came home, weary from the workshop.

4

The morning sun crept stealthily into the room through the cracks in the wooden window, sweeping away shadows in the dusty corners, alighting over Bablu's eyelids. He opened his eyes reluctantly and stretched himself with a sigh of contentment, exposing the two holes in his vest under the left armpit.

His mother and younger sister, Shalu, were both drinking tea in the kitchen and handed him a cup. Looking for his wife, he sauntered out to the back porch and saw Gowri walking hurriedly towards the bathroom, holding a bloodstained rag in her hand.

Concerned, he asked, 'Gowri, what happened? Did you cut your hand, show me!'

He caught her hand, taking the rag from

her before she could react. Flushing with embarrassment, his wife snatched her arm away. Bablu looked at her with surprise and at the bloodstained cloth in his hand. Understanding dawned in his eyes.

Gowri silently took the rag from him and went inside the bathroom. Later when she found him still in their room, she immediately busied herself, combing her wet hair in front of the small mirror on the wall, opening an orange plastic box filled with cream from the shelf next to it and rubbing it on her face.

He asked her, 'Gowri, can I ask you a question, that grubby cloth you had in your hand, is that what you use, you know, for that uh...ladies' problem?'

She nodded hesitantly and before he could ask her any more questions, his mother called out from the front porch, 'Bablu, I am going to Rachna's house, I might stay there tonight. Her husband has still not come back from Ahmedabad and Pintu has got chickenpox. Haan, listen, she was also asking if you can come there after you finish with the workshop, and fix her boiler?'

Bablu replied, 'Yes Ma, I will be there at six o'clock.' And then Bhairavi Kewat added, 'Arrey, Bablu, this dog of yours has made a big mess near the steps, ask Gowri to clean it!'

He good-naturedly muttered 'Yes Ma' before taking an old newspaper and heading out to clean up himself.

Cycling towards Dewas, where his workshop was located, he had to wait fifteen minutes at the traffic lights. The dented red bus ahead of him refused to move as the driver was involved in a screaming match with a rickshaw driver causing yet another traffic jam.

An old beggar woman, her hair dishevelled, skin covered in dust and wearing threadbare clothes, walked up to him. Feeling sorry for her, Bablu took out a one-rupee coin from his pocket and dropped it into the metal tin in her hand.

He watched her go to the autorickshaw standing next to him and engage in a long, hushed conversation with the driver. Just as she moved away, he heard the driver say, 'Yes Ma ji.' Curious, he asked the autorickshaw driver, 'You know her?'

The driver replied, 'Yes, she is the owner of this

rickshaw and has two more, she was telling me to park it under the shed tonight because it looks like it is going to rain.'

Bablu laughed. 'Bhaiya, what can I say except I think I am in the wrong business!'

Late for work, he quickly unlocked the shutters for the three employees waiting outside. He had joined the workshop six years ago, first as a busboy, getting tea and tobacco for the owner, Shantaram Seth, and then had slowly worked his way up to becoming a welder himself.

When Shantaram Seth had started drinking heavily, Bablu had not only ensured that Shantaram was safe in bed each night, even carrying him on his back after finding him lying inebriated on the side of the road, but had also gradually taken over the mortgage of the workshop. Over the last two years he had run the business himself, growing it steadily.

He enjoyed working with machines and though he had been an indifferent student at best he still remembered his science teacher's name, Mrs B. Sharma, and the egg incubator that he had made under her supervision.

But when Bablu's father died leaving his mother struggling to support her small family, he had dropped out of school to get a job and help her out.

Inherently a cheerful, optimistic man, he had no bitterness, reasoning with himself that, despite not finishing high school, he had not done badly for himself. He just had a few more payments to make to the moneylenders towards the mortgage and then he could save up and buy a brand-new scooter.

That evening on his way back from the workshop, Bablu decided to surprise Gowri with yet another gift. He stopped his cycle outside a small store with a lopsided signboard that proudly said G.K. Pundit and Sons. Walking up to the counter, he asked the store owner, 'Ganjkaran Bhaiya, I want to buy a packet of...of...that thing they use, that...' Trailing off, unsure of the exact words to use though he had seen the advertisements often enough on television.

A perspiring Ganjkaran put away the blue plastic flyswatter that he had been fanning himself with and sniggered, 'Bablu, just say condoms, wasting so much time stammering!' And he pulled out a small black packet labelled 'Kamasutra LongLast' depicting a man and a woman in the throes of passion. 'No Ganjkaran Bhaiya, that other packet, which ladies use, you know, that time of the month.' Ganjkaran smirked. 'Achha, sanitary pads! Wah, your wife has already made you her puppy and taught you to fetch and carry?'

Seeing Bablu's narrowed eyes and realizing that he had forgotten the most important rule of business, to be deferential to the customer, he added, 'Just a joke only! Tell me which brand you want?'

Bablu was confused. It had never occurred to him that there were brands to choose from and he asked Ganjkaran to give him whichever one the shopkeeper thought was the best.

Ganjkaran pulled out a packet from underneath the display counter that was filled with bars of Lux soap, blue plastic Parachute oil bottles and bundles of pens and pencils.

Wrinkling his nose distastefully as if he was handling the day-old carcass of a mangy cat, he quickly wrapped the packet in an old newspaper, looping a string around it several times before knotting it, and slipped it into a black plastic packet. Bablu was startled at the exorbitant price and dutifully took out forty rupees from his shirt pocket and paid him.

He began cycling towards his sister Rachna's house when it occurred to him that he should go and collect some neem leaves for his nephew Pintu, who had contracted chickenpox.

He recalled the time he had been ill with the dreaded infection as a child. He shuddered now at the memory of those ugly red scabs which had never stopped itching. His father had boiled some neem leaves in water and given Bablu a bath with the decoction. The neem leaves and his father's gentleness had soothed his irritated skin.

Ram Kewat had been a handloom weaver who worked primarily from home and unlike Bhairavi, who dominated the household with both affection and her fierce temper, he had been a softer soul. Nine years had passed since his father's death but rarely did a week go by without Bablu thinking of him.

He turned on to a narrow dirt road, the wild shrubs and vegetation getting denser as he ventured further. He reached the little clearing filled with neem trees and plucked two large handfuls of the small spiky leaves, stuffing them in the black packet holding the sanitary napkins.

As his hand brushed against the bulky packet, curiosity overtook him. He unwrapped the newspaper, tore open the plastic packaging and pulled out one of the cotton pads.

He examined the pad gingerly at first, like it was a strange new animal, one that would suddenly wake up and bite his hand. After turning it one way and the other, he decided that it seemed to be just plain cotton wrapped with a gauze sheet. He placed it on his palm, trying to calculate the approximate weight of the pad. 'Ten grams,' he said to himself.

Having seen his father working with cotton yarn through his childhood, he knew that ten grams of cotton would barely cost ten paise. But here he was paying four rupees for each of these pads. He put the sanitary pad back in its packet.

~

Bhairavi Kewat and Rachna were sitting on the porch steps. They were looking out at Rachna's little garden, past her broken gate, into the busy evening road filled with honking two-wheelers. Rachna grumbled, 'When is this Bablu ever on time? From our schooldays till now. I have to always wait for him.'

When her mother made a soothing gesture, Rachna continued, 'Oh Ma, I forgot to tell you – last Tuesday, when you had gone to Durga Masi's house, I was on my way to the market and stopped by the house.

'Gowri was just sitting and listening to the radio. I tell you, Ma – you should pull her up a little. You know how particular I am. When she was getting me water, I quickly ran my hand around the door jamb and on the windowsill and, will you believe it, my fingers were covered with dirt and grime. God knows what that woman does all day besides daydreaming!'

Before Bhairavi Kewat could reply, they spotted Bablu. He pushed open the broken gate and moved it back and forth before he walked up to the house. He said, 'The whole metal plate has broken into two. You should have told me, I will get the welding tools from the workshop and do it tomorrow. Now show me your precious boiler.'

He thrust the neem leaves into his mother's hands, examined the boiler and after fiddling with it for a few moments told his sister with a smile, 'It will work for now but I can't guarantee when it will break down again. I suggest you fast every Monday for its long life, only God can help your boiler after this.'

After reassuring his nephew who was playing Ludo with Shalu that soon all the itching, even inside his ears and nostrils, would subside, he made an excuse and quickly left Rachna's house. He was eager to get home and give his new wife her present.

5

'Close your eyes and give me your hand,' Bablu said. 'Here, now guess what I have got for you.'

Gowri ran her hands over the packet, her fingers grazing the newspaper as she began guessing. 'Is it a sari, is it the same blue one I showed you in the window at Jagannath Saris?' And she excitedly tore the newspaper wrapping and opened her eyes.

'Sanitary pads? And why is the packet torn?' she asked, perplexed.

Bablu was dismayed by Gowri's reaction. He mumbled, 'I opened the packet, had never seen a pad before. I thought you didn't know about sanitary pads. I got it for you, Gowri, so that you could use these only and not those dirty pieces of cloth.'

Gowri hesitantly replied, 'Of course I know

about pads. I have seen the same advertisements like you, a girl in a white dress jumping on the grass, but if Shalu and I start buying these packets every month, then let alone curd and ghee, we will not even have enough money to buy milk.'

Bablu looked at her dejectedly, his spirits sinking. Then she suddenly laughed, and her hand, almost of its own accord, reached towards him, touching his cheek delicately.

It had taken Gowri a few minutes to understand that Bablu in his own idiosyncratic way was trying to fill her life with small moments of joy that he could both envision and afford.

And disregarding all the old wives' tales about not being intimate during the days of menstruation, they made good use of Ma's and Shalu's absence, on the thick mattress, behind the floral bed sheet that served as the partition wall of their tiny bedroom.

The next day while the sun was still shining fiercely in the summer sky, Bablu pulled down and padlocked the metal shutters of the workshop. He then set off towards the main market.

On his way back, he took the diversion to the clearing with the neem trees to get some more leaves for his nephew and decided to sit there and work on his new project.

He pulled out a pair of scissors, a needle and some thread, cotton and muslin cloth from his bag and began flattening the cotton between his hands as if he were spreading out dough to make a chapatti. Taking two large leaves from a nearby tree, he placed the cotton between them, pressing firmly with his hands till it was flattened. He then wrapped the flattened cotton in the muslin cloth and stitched up all the corners. Within twenty-four hours of first touching a sanitary napkin, Bablu had managed to make his own.

Excited, he rushed home. Seeing his wife standing on the porch, waiting for him, he bounded up to her and placed his ingeniously crafted sanitary napkin in her hand. 'Gowri, go quickly, try this and tell me how it is. Those rascal multinationals are bloodsucking parasites, charging a fortune for just a bit of cotton. I have made this pad in less than fifty paise. Go on, try it!'

Gowri looked surprised but nodded. 'All right, but not now, maybe after a few weeks,' she said and walked towards the kitchen.

Bablu was bewildered. Walking behind her he pleaded, 'No, no, why after a few weeks, try it now!'

She turned towards him and replied, 'It is not a ceiling fan that I can switch on and off. It is over now, yesterday was the last day. You just have to wait till next month.'

6

The smoke from the effigy of Ravana and the sound of exploding fireworks filled the evening sky. It was Dussehra. The lanes of Mohana were crowded with people dressed in their finery, returning home after seeing the annual Ramlila performance.

Gowri was walking back home with Bablu and his friend Akram. The streets were dark and Bablu pointed out the silhouette of the moon hidden behind the clouds to Gowri. Akram, who along with being the neighbourhood butcher also happened to be its resident poet, began spouting one of his inane limericks:

'The beauty of the moon,
I say I am immune,
Because without the sun,
It is only a pebble, you baboon.'

Akram, realizing that his audience seemed unmoved, added, 'Bablu, now no one gives me my due importance but if I get my poems printed in the *Dainik Bhaskar*, by God, my name will be on everyone's lips in this town!'

Bablu put his arm around Akram's shoulder and replied, 'Akram Bhai, that is not a difficult accomplishment. Go borrow money from whomsoever you meet and then disappear. Hordes of people will walk around the market, saying, "Where is that bloody Akram?", "If you see that bastard Akram, let me know!", "If I catch Akram, I will stab him with his own knife!"'

Gowri, spotting Akram's dismayed face, stifled a giggle and Bablu, unable to control himself, burst out laughing as well.

After Akram had turned towards his house, Bablu and Gowri walked quietly together to their home. Their shoulders sometimes touched, their hands occasionally brushed against each other. The night felt quiet and intimate. The autumn wind was cool, making Gowri wish she had carried a shawl.

She asked Bablu, 'Achha, what is your favourite

colour? I am thinking of making a sweater for you, sleeveless or should I make one with long sleeves?' And she told him about her grandmother who would sit with her spooling ball of coloured wool, using the needles to both knit and poke people mercilessly when they were not paying attention to her.

Bablu laughed along with her. As they talked and teased one another, he realized that in the last few weeks he had completely forgotten to ask Gowri about his homemade pad. 'Gowri, did you try it? The pad?' he asked.

She didn't reply at first and then eventually said, 'Suno ji,' the way she always referred to him, 'yes, I tried it, it doesn't work; I had to wash my clothes in less than ten minutes. I know you are doing it to make me happy but please stop asking me about these things. It makes me very uncomfortable. These are women's matters, leave them to us.'

Bablu was astounded. Of all the eventualities that he had imagined as he amused himself while cycling up and down to his workshop – Gowri declaring that she could never have imagined that her husband was such a genius, of women all over India using sanitary napkins with his face printed on the packet and even having a temple made in his honour like they did of so many South Indian movie stars – he had not foreseen this easy dismissal of his creation.

'But why?' he spluttered. 'How can you feel comfortable using a dirty rag?'

Gowri murmured, 'Leave it. I am satisfied with my cloth – after all I have been using it all these years. It's what your mother and sisters do, what my mother does. Why think so much?'

'But do you like it, Gowri?' asked Bablu softly. 'Why should you feel satisfied? Isn't it unfair that you can't afford a simple…'

Gowri interrupted him, 'Let's stop fighting over this. I know you mean well. But these are not things that you should concern yourself with. Bas, no more now. Please? Promise me?'

He nodded at her and continued walking, seemingly undisturbed, changing the subject to the Ramlila performance. 'Did you notice, the man who played Lakshman's part was completely drunk, just stood there swaying on the side of the stage?' he asked his wife.

But the conversation had planted a seed in his mind.

The next day as Bablu unlocked the padlock that secured his cycle, he saw his neighbour's wife Parul in the small courtyard outside her house. She had a thin towel wrapped around her freshly washed hair as she took circles around the tulsi planted in a dingy white pedestal in the middle of her small garden. He called out a greeting to her and she nodded sullenly.

Six months ago, Choti had ventured into her garden and pulled out some of her marigold plants. Parul had come screaming into his house, threatening him, brandishing a broom in her hand like it was Tipu Sultan's sword.

Bablu tried to assure her that the incident would not be repeated, but Choti, fearing that the portly woman in the green sari with the broom raised in the air was posing a serious threat to her master, lunged at her, knocking her down. After that, despite Bablu's repeated apologies, she had refused to talk to him. A grudging nod with an under-the-breath cuss word was the most she would offer.

But his problems with Parul did not bother him today because he had something more important on his mind. Bablu with the same uncompromising determination that had taken him from being an errand boy to the owner of the workshop had just made a grand announcement to his wife, 'These rascal big corporations are only trying to cheat people, charging so much money for a simple cotton pad. You wait and see, Gowri, I will find a way to make a pad for you at quarter the price.'

7

Months passed with Bablu procuring different qualities of cotton and various materials to make new pads. He would then give each one to Gowri in the manner of a courtier presenting rare jewels to a king, only to watch Gowri proclaim all his experiments as wholly inadequate.

One evening as she was sitting on the back seat of his cycle, he broached the topic again. Gowri had tried to understand her husband but she was beginning to get impatient and upset about this unnatural obsession of his.

Trying hard not to show her annoyance, she said, 'Suno ji, would it not be more sensible to put in that much effort into earning more money so that we can just afford to buy sanitary pads every month?'

Bablu replied, 'I can try and earn more and buy an expensive packet of sanitary pads for my wife, but what about everyone else's wives?' He continued, 'I started with doing this just for you, Gowri, but after you rejected four pads I made with different grades of cotton, I went to a doctor's clinic in Dewas. I asked the compounder there for a sample of the cotton they used for dressings.

'I thought that perhaps it would be more absorbent than the samples I was finding. The compounder asked me what I wanted the cotton for and when I explained, he said, "Bhai saab, you are the first husband I have seen who has come into this clinic and even spoken about sanitary pads. Most women use dirty cloth, leaves and even straw and you know what – they have seventy per cent more chances of getting diseases. But no one seems to be bothered about these things."

'Seventy per cent, Gowri. It's such a big number. I thought about his words for days as I looked at the little girls running around our neighbourhood. They can't even buy an extra pair of slippers – how will they ever be able to afford sanitary pads from the market month after month?'

Gowri was silent for a few moments and then said, 'I pray that no such diseases will come upon those girls but let their fathers and husbands look after them. Your responsibility lies towards our family, our future.'

And trying to avoid any further discussion, she said, 'Suno ji, this Sunday let's go see a movie in the cinema, please,' and Bablu nodded and cycled on. He didn't raise the subject all evening and Gowri hoped his silence was a good sign.

But Bablu remained single-minded, despite her best efforts. Each month he would present her a new pad to try, each month she would ask him to discontinue his experiments.

Once this man had come bearing her sweet gifts, small tokens that had opened the doors of her heart to him. But now continually dealing with the onslaught of his unseemly obsession, she felt that she didn't know him any more.

Slowly, the delicate intimacy that had begun to grow between the couple began to turn into an invisible chasm instead.

But Bablu faced a larger problem than his wife's mounting frustration – and this was her menstrual cycle. In order to get feedback on his pads he had to wait an entire month. One day, he loudly exclaimed, 'Gowri! At this rate it will take me decades to get this right.'

Unable to take it any more, she began sobbing. 'I don't know what sins I must have done in my past life that all this is happening! I am not going to try any pad or anything any more. At least then you will have to stop this madness.'

Bablu then began pestering his sisters to try his sanitary pads. Unfortunately, during a family lunch, his nephew Pintu accidentally pulled a sanitary pad out of Bablu's bag and began waving it like a flag in front of the entire gathering, including Uma ji, an elderly lady from the neighbourhood who had dropped in to invite Bhairavi Kewat to her granddaughter's wedding.

Bhairavi tried to make light of the matter not wanting to create a scene in front of an outsider, but after Uma ji left, Rachna berated her brother and along with their mother beseeched him to stop his experiments saying that the whole family would be disgraced due to his sordid interest in women's menstrual cycles.

But the damage was already done. Uma ji quickly spread the news about Bablu being a pervert who carried sanitary napkins in his pocket and soon the whole town was talking about him and treating him as the local pariah.

They did not spare the rest of the family either, entangling them in a mesh of coarse whispers and contemptuous glances.

A few days later when Bablu was cycling back home from the workshop, he spotted Akram standing at Madhukar's tea stall. Akram called out to him and Bablu stopped his cycle and joined his friend. Akram had just returned from Lucknow the previous evening and began to regale his friend with his adventures there.

In the middle of his stories, he realized that his friend seemed rather gloomy. 'What is the matter, Bablu?' he asked, seeing his friend staring vacantly at his tea. 'Is everything all right?'

'Akram Bhai, what is the point of telling you? You can't help me with this. I desperately need to find some women now.'

Akram smirked. 'Bablu, you are a married man and if you feel like this, what do you think must be happening to bachelors like us?'

Bablu just smiled, shook his head and explained his dilemma to Akram. Now that his family was not cooperating, where would he find any women who would openly discuss menstruation, let alone give him details about leakages, odours and soaking properties after using his sanitary pads?

Akram patted him on the back. Though he sympathized with his friend, he could not resist making a joke at his expense: 'Arrey Bablu, God should have made you a woman, then it would have been so much easier to just test the pads yourself.'

But his little joke sparked an idea in Bablu's mind. He roped a reluctant Akram into his project, asking him to give him some fresh goat's blood for testing. When the blood clotted almost instantly, Bablu went back to the compounder at the doctor's clinic in Dewas, who suggested the use of an anticoagulant.

They then added this to the next batch and Bablu was finally ready. He had managed to assemble as realistic a uterus as he could with his rubber bladder filled with blood and a plastic tube.

It was this that had led to the unfortunate incident at the well, and the ensuing infamy. Gowri, unable to bear the humiliation, finally left him – saying she would only return when he had given up his madness.

Bablu Kewat had reached a point in his life where he had lost his wife, his friends, money that he could ill afford to waste and, as the world believed, his mind, all in pursuit of the sanitary pad project.

But all these losses seemed only to strengthen his resolve. He was now on a path where his salvation lay in succeeding. If he stopped midway he would forever be branded a lunatic at best, if not a bloodthirsty vampire with sexual perversions.

8

It was a pleasant Sunday morning and Bhairavi Kewat had come with Shalu to Rachna's house in a disturbed state. She was at her wits' end about how to deal with Bablu. It had been three months since Gowri had left for her parents' home. Bablu had got paler and thinner and quieter in these months but hadn't stopped working on his project.

She had tried cajoling him, screaming at him and had even put on a mighty good show of having chest pains. But Bablu had promptly called Vaidya ji, the Ayurvedic doctor, from the market, who after checking her pulse had declared, 'Behan ji, you have a lot of gas in your system,' and had prescribed pills for indigestion.

Rachna too had her own complaints about Bablu. She had gone across to talk to him but he refused to listen to her and said, 'Rachna, since you are so interested in my well-being, tell me, are your periods due soon? Try my new pads and fill out all the details on this feedback sheet, please.'

Leaving Shalu behind to help Rachna with a few chores, Bhairavi Kewat left her daughter's house in a confused state of mind.

She had always ruled her little household decisively and firmly, leaving very little rope for her children to trip over. But now she felt like she was in the middle of a whirlwind she couldn't control. Gowri's absence, the neighbours and their taunts, her son who seemed to have lost his mind, it all seemed too much for her.

Bablu had not just been her favourite child, but had also been her strongest support all through the years when both mother and son had worked endless hours to ensure the survival of their small family.

He had always been such a good child and, unlike Rachna and Shalu, had never demanded anything. She recalled the joy on his face when on rare occasions she made kheer for him, the way he would nestle up next to her even as a twenty-year-old, his head on her lap, telling her amusing anecdotes about his customers at the workshop. She did not understand how things had suddenly shifted, what had led to the utter wreckage of their happy world.

She wearily pushed open the creaky gate to her house and walked inside. The door to the backyard was open and she saw Bablu sitting on the floor, a handkerchief tied around his nose.

At first glance, she thought he was chopping chicken for their Sunday lunch but as she came closer the smell sent her reeling. Her beloved son was sitting on the grass with dozens and dozens of used sanitary napkins that he had picked out of the bins from a girls' hostel spread out around him. She watched in disbelief as he picked one up, peered at it and then dropped it only to pick up another.

Bhairavi Kewat had a sobbing fit and within the hour she too had packed Shalu's bags along with her own and left to go live with Durga Masi.

9

The days passed with a pensive Bablu cycling to the workshop and coming back to an empty house. His heart was filled with bleakness but his work continued. His first priority was to find out the exact specifications of the material used by the big corporations for their pads. On a cotton trader's recommendation, he had sent the multinational company's pads to a lab for testing. They sent him a letter stating: Material found to be cellulose. But none of the cotton traders he asked knew anything about this material.

Desperate for information, he impulsively decided to call a college professor living in Indore.

Bhaskar Sharma was a relative so distant that he was tied to the family tree only by the frayed rakhis that Bablu's long-departed chachi had tied on to his wrist annually on Raksha Bandhan during their childhood years in Mohana.

Professor Sharma, an elderly gentleman who had managed to retain his thick hair except for a small balding spot at the back that he carefully covered each morning, worked in the sociology department at the Indian Institute of Technology.

He picked up the insistently ringing phone and at first had trouble trying to figure out exactly how Bablu claimed to be related to him. But there is a mysterious part of every Indian's heart that regards anyone from his home town as a member of his extended family. So the good professor decided to hear out this nervous-sounding man.

Bablu poured his heart out to the sympathetic voice on the other end of the line. The professor found himself deeply moved by his story. Impressed with Bablu's perseverance and his own curiosity stimulated, he spent days scouring the Internet and finally managed to get hold of a few details of a factory that supplied cellulose to Procter & Gamble. He then sent them an email on Bablu's behalf and also gave him the factory's telephone number.

Bablu was not well versed in English, though he could read a little and communicate in broken bits. Unable to contain his eagerness at finally making some progress, he hurriedly called the number, pretending to be a wealthy textile mill owner in Indore.

'Hello, I myself Mr Prabhash Kewat, textile mill owner this side, I wrote mail also, request kindly for sample of raw material.'

A high-pitched voice replied, 'Hello sir, this is Miranda Davis from the business development department. I have been through your email, sir. If I may ask, how large is your plant?'

Bablu wondered about the relevance of this question and replied, 'Madam, I have many plants tulsi plant, champa plant, ashoka plant, katkal plant, you want size of which one?'

There was a long pause and Bablu, wondering if he had given himself away, waited anxiously for her reply.

Fortunately, these bizarre answers only strengthened Ms Davis's impression that he was indeed a prosperous businessman who just had some language issues. She promptly dispatched the samples to the address he had given her. A few weeks later they reached Mohana.

10

The brown cardboard box lay forlornly near the kitchen stove. Bablu, standing beside it, was carefully chopping onions for some poha. He was puzzled. The samples he had received were not cotton at all, but some mysterious strips of hardboard. He looked despondently at the boards lying on the tiled floor, not quite knowing what to make of them.

Choti was barking incessantly in the backyard and Bablu went to check on her. The dog had spotted Parul picking up dry clothes from the washing line in her backyard and was now trying to leap over the wall to get at her. Parul sneered triumphantly at the sight of Bablu, rotating her index finger in slow circles next to her right temple. 'Bablu and his dog, both mental!' She laughed mockingly as she walked back into her house.

Bablu sat down gloomily on the steps leading to the backyard. Choti bounded up to him and, after nuzzling his arm and wagging her tail around her master for a few moments, bounded inside the house but Bablu didn't move. He felt a heaviness in his chest. After all this time and after so many sacrifices, he had still not discovered what was used to make sanitary pads.

He glanced in the direction of Parul's backyard, now empty aside from a fluttering peacock-blue sari. Perhaps she was right in calling him mental, for his pursuits had only brought catastrophe to his door. He had been certain that he would finally succeed this time and then with his head held high he would bring his family back home.

He sighed heavily and, placing his hands on his pyjama-clad legs for support, as if he had aged decades while sitting on the steps, he slowly pushed himself up and shuffled inside the house to finish preparing his meal.

He sliced the green chillies inexpertly into uneven pieces and, looking out of the kitchen window, saw the first raindrops splattering on the grass outside.

The monsoons had been late this year but were finally here. Not that all the rain in the world could wash away his troubles.

He glanced once again at the worthless boards, but he saw only one. That Choti, the rascal, must have carried the other away. Bablu went out to the front porch and, sure enough, Choti had the mangled board in front of her, one end chewed, and with her long nails she had scratched the board all over.

Bablu picked up the board and looked at it carefully. The scratches had ripped the top layer of the board and he could see a white downy material that had been compressed into the form of the board. They had sent him the raw material pressed into sheets.

And as he would soon realize from the contents of an email that had been sent to Professor Sharma asking for confirmation of delivery, it was not cotton at all, which is why his pads had never worked efficiently – it was wood pulp cellulose from the bark of the pine tree.

Bablu had found the magic ingredient but as Professor Sharma said to him over the phone that evening, 'Kewat, I think you should let it go now. The machines that the large corporations use to break down this material and turn it into sanitary napkins cost crores of rupees. Some trees are impossible to climb no matter what ambrosial fruit hangs from their branches.'

But Bablu wasn't going to give up when he had just made a small victory. Full of optimism, he replied, 'Professor saab, sometimes you have to carve your own footholds in the trunk as you go along.' So Bablu decided he would just have to try to make the machine himself.

11

It was a muggy night and the heat and the swarms of pests that thronged the stifling shanty located in the by-lanes of Indore made a restless Bablu toss and turn on the mattress that he shared with Choti.

The headman, along with the rest of the panchayat of Mohana, had, despite Bhairavi Kewat's pleas, eventually given him an ultimatum. He had to accept either their stringent exorcism rites or banishment from the town.

Bablu knew that the chances of surviving hanging upside down from a tree for an indefinite number of days, while bearing lashings and being doused with boiling water, and the swallowing of obscure potions, all in order to drive the devil out of his body, would be rather dim, especially since he was certain that the only thing that seemed to be rattling inside him was a sense of purpose and some common sense. But he knew it was no good trying to convince the town council.

He immediately vacated his house in Mohana and sold his workshop, sending a significant part of the money to his mother, who was still staying with Durga Masi. He then moved to Indore and with the leftover money rented a shed with a tin roof that multitasked as a workshop during the day and a gloomy bedroom at night.

He had tried calling his mother a few times, but all the telephone calls ended with her weeping, which would disturb him for days on end. Finally, the day before he was leaving for Indore, he called her again, but Durga Masi picked up the phone and she firmly told her nephew that he had done enough damage and he should now spare the family from any further humiliation. That was the day Bablu realized that he had been totally cast aside by his loved ones.

He had not heard from Gowri in all this time and under these circumstances where he possessed nothing to offer her, not even a home, he had tried to push her out of his mind. But ever so often when he thought about her and his mother and sisters, the loneliness and hurt sometimes gnawed at him so furiously that he could feel it rattling inside his chest, clawing to get out with each breath.

He sat up, scratching his armpit which seemed to be a rare and delicious delicacy as far as the mosquitoes were concerned, and looked at the four small machines on the table in front of him.

It had taken him almost two years from the day he had first held the wood pulp boards in his hands. Two years that he had spent largely at this workshop, taking up odd welding jobs during the day to eke out a living and weary nights building his machines.

Undeterred by the size and complexities of the machines in the mammoth factories that produced sanitary napkins, Bablu had tried to unravel the process to its bare bones. He needed to begin with finding a way to break down the hardboard of the wood pulp.

He had tried to first make an electric machine attaching four table forks to the tip, forks that moved horizontally back and forth, trying to mechanically replicate Choti's actions. After spending three fruitless months which resulted in ruining one board as well as rewarding Bablu with a tear on his right arm that required five stitches, he abandoned that line of pursuit.

A few weeks later, Bablu was installing grills in a small flat. The lady of the house was hovering between supervising him and getting lunch ready. During a short break, he sat on the tiled kitchen floor, gratefully sipping on the hot sugary tea that she had given him, watching her tossing coconut, roasted chana dal, chopped ginger, green chilli and oil into a blender jar, the kitchen brimming with the intermittent whistles from her pressure cooker and the whirring noise of the electric mixer-grinder.

Taking the bus back to his workshop that evening, the image of the swivelling blades of the mixer filled his head and he started working on a simple machine with modified parts of a high-powered blender.

After months of trial and error, he finally succeeded in making a small machine that could break down the cellulose board, safely and effectively.

His next task lay in taking the fibrous mass and flattening and assembling it into a rectangular cake, the shape of a sanitary pad.

This turned out to be the simplest process. Taking inspiration from soap moulds and watching the rotund, vest-clad dhobi across the street ironing and pressing disobediently creased bed sheets into neat flattened piles, he made his second machine.

Then he devised a third apparatus that worked like a mechanical rotating toilet paper holder that wrapped his pads. Now he faced one last hurdle – the hardest of all. How would he ensure that the sanitary pads he made were not actually unsanitary?

That week, sitting on the rattan chair across Professor Sharma, who had turned out to be his only support during the last few years, Bablu finally wept. The abandonment by his family, living on the floor of his workshop, even the lack of a decent, home-cooked meal, and now this latest impediment in his progress, had mounted one challenge on top of the other. His despair was finally eating into his resolve.

Professor Sharma looked at the young man who had cast aside his entire world because of a single idea, and felt a rush of deep compassion towards him. The professor had seen so much of himself in Bablu, as a man struggling to rise above the terrain of his birth. Bablu's defeats felt like his, the young man's advances, his victories.

He made Bablu stay for dinner and promised to look up the most efficient way of disinfecting the sanitary napkins and assured Bablu that he would ask his colleagues at the institute as well. With Mrs Sharma heaping his plate with her spicy dal and towering piles of aloo puri, and the professor's calm reassurance, Bablu's spirits began to rise again.

Six months later, he had completed and tested the four machines he required for the manufacture of his sanitary pads. They were a round appliance, fitted with the parts of a modified kitchen grinder that would break down the hardboard; a core forming machine that turned the fluffy fibres into a rectangular cake using moulds and an electric press; a finishing roller where the cakes were wrapped; and an elementary contraption used at the final stage that disinfected the pads with ultraviolet light.

Bablu waved the mosquitoes away and decided to get out of bed. He walked across to the table that held his four precious machines and began carefully packing each one with bubble wrap and styrofoam before lowering them into cardboard boxes.

On Professor Sharma's recommendation, he was going to take his low cost sanitary napkin making invention for a demonstration at the Indian Institute of Technology.

12

The rain splattered against the weathered wooden shutters, splashing on to the iron grills. It dampened Gowri's hair as she sat against the window, peering outside at the ripples on the green pond filled with mottled green leaves and a squawking black duck.

She recalled sitting with Bablu on a rainy day just like this, brooding over a remark her mother-in-law had carelessly tossed on their way back from the market the previous evening. Bhairavi Kewat, walking arm in arm with Rachna, had said, 'Gowri, you should really follow Rachna's example, she learned just by watching me and is such a good cook now!'

Gowri had returned home crestfallen and Bablu had tried to placate her later, as they leaned against the railing of the porch steps. He said laughing, 'Ma is right; Rachna has been a good cook since childhood! She could always fry people's brains, make their blood boil and cut them into tiny pieces without using any equipment except her tongue, how can anyone compete with that!'

Sitting under the grey, stormy skies, Gowri, who had never seen her husband despondent, recalled asking him, 'How are you always so upbeat?' And he, the colour of burnished cinnamon, had smirked and said, 'I always carry a little sunshine within my skin, madam.'

Bablu with his silly antics and generous heart had made a place for himself in Gowri's life. She had left Mohana thinking that he would come to his senses, stop all his bizarre experiments. With that, all the malicious talk about him would also come to an end and he would come and take her back. But though she kept waiting, he never tried to contact her.

13

The hall with its white panelled ceiling, fluorescent tube lights and uncomfortable-looking brown chairs was filled with faculty and students from various departments. Bablu was waiting for Dr Chattopadhya to finish a lecture on 'micro optical devices for optical logic, interconnects and signal processing' after which there would be a short break for refreshments and then he and his sanitary pad manufacturing machine would have their five minutes in the spotlight.

He had nervously finished assembling his machines backstage and was munching on a Glucose biscuit when two men in suits standing next to him began a conversation. Dr Gupta, the bespectacled, swarthy man, began by saying, 'Mehta, I am scheduled to give a talk at 3 p.m.

on correlations between insulin resistance and C-peptide. And you?'

The other man replied that his talk was scheduled for the following day. Dr Gupta turned to Bablu, taking in his old grey pants, the blue shirt through which his white vest was visible, and his Bata rubber slippers, and said, 'Aye boy, get us some tea.'

Bablu, his ears burning, did not reply and finally murmured, 'Sir, I am also here to present my machine.' Dr Gupta looked at Bablu with scepticism and asked him which institute he belonged to. Bablu replied, 'Sir, I have not been to any institute but I am eight standard pass from Saraswati Vidyalaya, Mohana.' Dr Gupta murmured to his colleague, 'Mehta, do some pest control on your campus. God knows what kind of uneducated idiots are walking around here!'

Bablu struggled to control his temper for a moment and then with his peculiar brand of self-possession directed a disarming smile at Dr Gupta and in his impeccable Hindi replied, 'Sir, I am uneducated but I am not an idiot. Idiots think that because something is complicated, it is superior, whereas an intelligent man takes a complicated thing and makes it simple. I am a simple man who has made a simple machine, now, sir, you do the rest of the calculations.'

He walked away, only to return with a cup of tea which he handed over to Dr Gupta, chuckling. 'Simple way to get tea – just a quick walk to the refreshments table. People unnecessarily make it so complicated.'

Ten minutes later, Bablu Kewat presented his invention on stage along with price comparisons between his finished product and the ones made by conglomerates, with an engineering student translating his words into English. His presentation was received with thunderous applause.

That evening Professor Sharma called the workshop asking Bablu how the presentation had gone. Bablu replied, 'It went well, though there was a man standing on the side, like the narrator of some stage play, translating everything I said. I think I really need to learn English properly now, Professor saab. It will really help me, if my English improves then I will be able to use the Internet also to look things up myself and not trouble you all the time.'

Professor Sharma too had only studied in Hindi during his years in Mohana and he recalled his agonizing struggle to catch up as a student at Jineshwar English Medium School in the ninth grade when his father had moved the family to Indore.

He gave Bablu the number of his grandson's tutor, Sarita Jagpal, who conducted group as well as individual after-school classes nearby.

14

The dusty black scooter stopped in front of the peeling building called Palatial Towers. Sarita parked it in one corner of the compound as her daughter Maina, her school bag dangling over one shoulder and her Mickey Mouse water bottle slung around her neck, jumped off the back seat.

Sarita hurried across the dilapidated lobby carefully opening the iron lattice door that always seemed ready to trap unsuspecting fingers, and stepped into the creaky elevator. It had been a long day, and the traffic had been especially bad.

She jabbed the seventh-floor button three times before the lift conceded to take them up. She had fifteen minutes to splash some water on her face and get a cup of tea, before her first student of the day would appear at her doorstep.

Sarita's BA in English had not quite opened doors to a teaching job at a well-known school as she had imagined. Instead it had landed her a place as the overqualified and underpaid supervisor, errand girl and general dogsbody at the embroidery unit located in the stifling garage that belonged to her employer, Mandira Sidhwani.

She supplemented her income and satisfied her desire to be part of India's education system by taking evening tuition classes, the regular middle school mathematics and science, along with a subject called 'Talking First Class English' as she had once seen it peculiarly advertised in the classified section of a newspaper.

In a country that was still reeling from a hangover of its colonial days, intelligence was determined not as much by a person's acumen as by their fluency in the English language – albeit a strange version consisting of phrases that would make the pale-faced British go red in the face like 'Entry from backside only'. So there was more than adequate demand for her classes.

Handing Maina a banana and her dog-eared copy of *The Jataka Tales*, she had brewed some tea when the doorbell rang. On the other side of the door, beaming his gap-toothed smile towards her, was her ten-year-old student Arvind Sharma and just behind him stood a tall man with a thin moustache and a nervous demeanour.

It was the new student Professor Sharma had recommended. Usually she taught schoolchildren. This would certainly be different, she thought to herself, looking at the nondescript man in front of her.

Bablu walked into the small living room and sat at the chipped wooden table she indicated with a wave. Arvind promptly sat by his side, hoisting his school bag on to the table, and began taking out his books.

Bablu looked at the delicate-looking woman across the table in the blue salwar kameez, her spectacles slipping off the bridge of her nose which she pushed back up with her index finger repeatedly.

He began with the one sentence in English he felt confident of – 'I myself Prabhash Kewat this side.' At which Sarita, looking amused, replied, 'Which side is that? This side of the Indian border or that side of the Pakistan one? This sentence is wrong.'

Taken aback, Bablu replied in Hindi, 'How, madam? If you are on that side of the table, then I am naturally on this side!'

Arvind started giggling and Sarita smiled. 'I can see that I have my work cut out for me. And please call me Sarita.' Giving Arvind a sheet of word problems to solve, Sarita pulled out an alphabet chart along with a printed sheet that stated 'Lesson 2 – English Greetings, Introductions and Farewells' and began tutoring Bablu.

15

Trucks and jeeps with blaring music and screeching slogans were whizzing by. Enjoying the December air, Bablu was sitting on the broad step of his workshop with Kailash Sahu, who owned the adjacent restaurant, Mehfil, famous for its bhutte ki kheer, a delicacy of grated fresh corn, pan-fried in ghee, milk and sugar.

Aditya Joshi, a junior officer at the Census office in Bhopal, making his customary trip through Indore, was also leaning against the workshop wall beside them.

Though it was not yet seven in the evening Kailash was already drinking from a bottle of strong-smelling country liquor while Bablu and Aditya Joshi were drinking cup after cup of watery tea made with the same tea leaves that had started their duty at seven that morning at the tea stall adjacent to the workshop.

Yet another truck passed by with a loudspeaker blaring 'Vote for Sailesh Singh Pawar, Vote for BJP!' Pointing at the truck, Kailash asked, 'Bablu, what do you think, who will win the election this year?'

Bablu answered, 'What is there to think, three times this crook Pawar has won and this year too victory will be his.'

Aditya Joshi interjected, 'Oof! Bablu Bhaiya, it is good if the Bharatiya Janata Party wins! See, under this government, population of full and final Madhya Pradesh grew only by twenty per cent and under the Congress party leadership it was growing at twenty-four per cent, so we have made good progress, na?'

Bablu replied, 'Aditya Bhai, the population has stabilized not because of the government but because of cable television operators. They are the ones responsible for controlling the population explosion by luring couples into watching blockbuster movies all Sunday long instead of thinking about procreation.

'This method of population control is a lot more effective than your government's policies. They only distributed free condoms thinking this would do the trick but the grateful citizens carefully saved all the condoms, only to use them as water balloons during Holi.'

Aditya Joshi looked over his shoulder at the small sanitary making unit that Bablu had installed in the workshop, having given up welding in order to concentrate on his new venture. He said, 'Bablu Bhaiya, you should pray that both the cable company continues showing hit movies and that the grateful citizens use condoms for the purpose it is made. Otherwise no one will buy your sanitary napkins, cheap or otherwise!'

Puzzled, Bablu asked, 'Why?'

'Bablu Bhaiya, because then all the ladies will get pregnant, na?' said Aditya Joshi and was greeted by Kailash's chortling laughter which was interrupted by the ringing of the workshop phone.

It was Professor Sharma in a state of high excitement. 'Kewat, good news!' he exclaimed. 'IIT had entered your machine for the National Innovation Awards after hearing your presentation.

Your low cost sanitary napkin machine has come first in the engineering category. You should be very proud – there were nine hundred and forty-three entries!'

Bablu felt dizzy with happiness. His pulse was racing and all he could croak out was 'I can't believe this, Professor saab! How did all this happen?'

The professor replied, 'There were many entries, how to extract gold from seawater, reach Mars by a shorter route, use dung for car fuel – all ideas and theories in spiral-bound notebooks and CDs. Yours was the only machine presented and with a strong social implication.

'One more thing, Kewat. You must apply for a patent for your invention as soon as possible, this country is full of untalented lazy scoundrels who are happy to bathe in a tub filled with another man's sweat. Come home tomorrow and we'll discuss the details.'

Though this threw up a rather unhygienic visual, Bablu who was now habituated to the good professor's flowery analogies assured him that he would be at the professor's house the very next evening.

179

16

Gowri was standing with her younger sister, Vijaya, inside the Narasimha Mandir. It was crowded with devotees offering flowers, fruits and coins.

The two sisters rang the bells of the temple, bowed down till their foreheads touched the mosaic temple floor and said a silent prayer to the idol in front of them.

Gowri, as always, thought of her absent husband and asked Lord Vishnu for guidance during this difficult phase of her life. She then took circles around the peepal tree in the temple courtyard and quietly moved towards the gate.

On the way back, Gowri was unusually quiet and when her sister questioned her, she said, 'I was just thinking about the time I had gone with him to a Hanuman ji temple in Ujjain. Everyone had been talking about the great miracle there. We were looking at the large idol of Hanuman ji. It was magnificent, life size, his crown was glistening gold and he had the most gentle eyes.

'The temple resounded with cries of "Jai Bajrang Bali" and the pandit ji put a coconut inside Hanuman ji's mouth. Hanuman ji shut his mouth and in a few seconds crushed coconut appeared from his silk-draped arm on to his open palm as prasad.

'I said to your brother-in-law, "This is so wonderful. Come quickly, let us also buy a coconut and get our blessings." And he laughed at me saying, "Gowri, it is wonderful but it is not god, just a machine. Instead of teeth there is a hammer inside Hanuman ji's mouth that crushes the coconut and then a pipe takes those pieces through his arm."

'I scolded him and he started teasing me, "Oh Gowri, put batteries in a torch and you can illuminate a room but it doesn't mean that a small star has fallen from the sky. And when you plug a radio into the socket, do you think Kishore

Kumar's ghost circles around the house haunting you with his singing? But you know, I would love to open it from the back and see how it works, very well made, I must say."

'Vijaya, I got so worried that he was uttering all this blasphemy that I shut my ears and started chanting the Hanuman Chalisa. But after a few days he got a toy car from the market, the kind that you turn a key on the side and it scoots forward, and with parts of a doll and old clocks, he made something similar, a puppet that would swallow a gooseberry and crack it into bits.'

Vijaya replied, 'Didi, you talk about him all the time. Why don't you send him a letter and tell him to come and fetch you? He is still your husband after all.'

Gowri murmured, 'I can't tell you how much I regret leaving Mohana. I wanted to run away from all the innuendos and pointing fingers, but is this any better? All the women here also look at me peculiarly because I am without a husband and I am fed up with all their smug whispers of "Poor Gowri" and "What will happen to Gowri!"

But where will I send my letter, Vijaya? No one knows where he is. Some people say he has gone to Bihar, some say he lives in Indore, but no one has an address, a contact number, nothing.'

17

Bablu Kewat and his unique invention were both aboard the Indore Dehradun Express. Bablu, with his head reclining against the window, was reading the newspaper, his stomach satiated with the two hot samosas that he had consumed ten minutes ago at Vikram Nagar station. As it happens on train journeys, the stranger on the opposite berth started an innocuous conversation with him.

Prashant Batra – 'But call me Prat' – had a strange low hairline that began almost with his bushy eyebrows. He was a freelance journalist who, having finished a story about the Kumbh Mela in Ujjain for the *Guardian*, had decided to spend a few days white-water rafting at Rishikesh before heading to Delhi.

Leaning towards Bablu, he began complaining

about the condition of the train toilet. Bablu was happy to participate in his still feeble English, starting with the one line he had now meticulously practised, 'My name is Prabhash Kewat. Nice to meet you.'

'Look, Prat Bhai,' he said smiling, 'don't see toilet as toilet. See it as a device designed by our kind and great government to benefit both the citizens and the country by helping Indians gain immunity from many diseases while simultaneously controlling population. When you enter the train toilet, all germs of full India are waiting to play kabaddi with you inside and in the beginning you may get dysentery or cholera or something.

'If you die, then population control, and if you survive then you will have best health because after this toilet-style of vaccination you will be immune to all germs. A win–win situation, Prat Bhai!'

Prashant Batra rubbed the sweat off his neck and started laughing at this eccentric man full of strange sagacity. 'You work for the government?'

Bablu laughed. 'No, I have done many things in my life, but never a job where people try to do as little as they can for as long as they can! I manufacture low cost sanitary napkins.'

Sensing a good story, Prashant Batra pushed Bablu to tell him more, opening his thermos and pouring them some sweet milky tea.

And so Bablu began his long tale of trials and tribulations and his triumph when he won the innovations award a year ago. He told the journalist that after getting a patent on the machine, he had slowly realized the potential of what he had in his hands.

'I had a choice, Prat Bhai, I could sell my patent to another company and make money or I could do something for the women in this country. One day, one of my employees brought his cousin, Bharti, to meet me. He said that she desperately needed a job. She was a tiny woman with uncombed hair, a torn blouse and a faded sari.

'I hired her and after six months I began to see changes. She had a new sari, her son began to go to school. I also realized that my customers felt more comfortable talking to a woman about their menstrual issues.

'I began to observe that when a woman's

economic status improves, her entire family's condition improves, whereas for a man that may not necessarily hold true.

'He will spend on himself, buy a new bike, spend on drinks and friends but a woman will spend all her money on her children. And that is when I decided that I would sell my machines only to women so that they could start their own sanitary pad making units and earn their livelihoods along with making low cost sanitary napkins accessible to the women in their neighbourhoods.'

Bablu then recounted his first forays in Bihar, where he had made his early contacts with the help of a cotton trader. 'I spoke to women, no, Prat Bhai, not about menstruation directly, otherwise all the Bihari babus would have made sure that I would be the one using a sanitary pad once again, this time as a bandage for my bleeding nose. I spoke to them about earning a livelihood, bas, they were all excited.

'I began selling my machines to groups of women, these women employed other women and they started their own sanitary napkin making units. They supplied the pads to ladies in their neighbourhood sometimes for money, sometimes in exchange for eggs and onion.

'And today many of them are completely independent. You know that saying, even a cat becomes a lioness in her own lair? These women are now roaring from their well-padded caves,' he laughed. 'I want to replicate this model in different states now and I want to try it in Uttarakhand next.'

Prashant had been listening in stunned silence to this extraordinary story. He said, 'Well done! So you took sanitary napkins and turned them into a security blanket also for women!'

Bablu was puzzled. 'Why in the world would I make napkins and then stitch them up as a blanket when I can just buy a ready-made blanket from Moolchand Market for seventy-five rupees? No, Prat Bhai! You didn't understand what I was saying!'

Laughing loudly, Prashant stood up and said, 'I have understood, my friend, but now please excuse me for a few moments.' He pulled out a roll of toilet paper from his haversack and, with a bottle of water and a bar of Lux soap proffered by Bablu, went to test his olfactory nerves, sanity and sense of balance in the train toilet.

The train lurched to the left and Prashant Batra staggered to one side, his leg precariously close to landing inside the toilet bowl. He tried to swiftly pull his pants up in order to get out of this rattling death trap and ended up dropping his mobile phone and a bunch of coins from the back pocket of his khaki chinos down the chute while just about managing to hold on to his wallet in the front pocket.

A disgruntled Prashant returned to his compartment and when he told Bablu about his mishap Bablu pulled out his newly purchased bulky Ericsson phone from his battered briefcase and said, 'Don't worry, Prat Bhai, what is mine is also yours. Use any time when both God and mobile tower next bless us with signal.'

Hours later, when Bablu got off at Dehradun station, Prashant also hauled his luggage out, deciding to accompany his new friend on his trip to the mountain village.

Fate had dropped Bablu Kewat in his lap and he knew he had a real story on his hands, one that the world would want to know about. As he told Bablu when the two men got off the train, 'Life is but a play of chance in the game of choice.'

18

Asha Rani Nautiyal was standing outside her hut, her forehead furrowed with worry and her small eyes narrowed into thin slits.

She buttoned her burgundy sweater tightly over her salwar kameez, bracing herself for the inevitable argument that would follow when she asked her husband for money.

She walked into the hut prepared to confront him and ended up confronting his bare backside instead. Her husband was drunk as usual, and he was lying comatose, with his underpants tangled between his knees and his worn-out brown sweater rolled high over his stomach. The room was filled with the stench of urine and liquor. She shook him awake.

Ridhim Nautiyal opened his bleary, red-rimmed eyes slowly. Annoyed at being woken up, he pulled up his pants, hurled a volley of abuses at Asha Rani and, catching her by her long, wavy hair with one hand, began raining blows on her head till she managed to push him away and run out of the hut. There would be no getting money out of him today.

Asha wearily walked towards her three-year-old son playing in the mud next to their meagre menagerie of goats and a few stray chickens. She looked over at the small fruit and vegetable field that she had cultivated behind her house, hoping that the shrivelled scarecrow in the middle was large enough to scare the monkeys away from the fruit-laden guava tree.

She pulled her son on to her lap, pulled off his woollen cap and started removing lice from his hair, killing each bloodsucking pest between her thumbnails with a sharp clicking sound.

The door opened and her husband shuffled out. Throwing a cursory glance in their direction, he headed towards the narrow road that led to the village centre. She didn't know if he would be back for dinner or if it would be days before he returned.

The sky changed to a pink and gold twilight. Asha Rani sat still, watching the day fade, the sleeping child bundled in her lap. Tilting her bruised face towards the snowy mountain peaks, she wondered if God had anything else in store for her besides grinding her down day after day, till there was nothing left but bone and gristle.

19

Bablu and Prashant arrived at the sarpanch's courtyard that also doubled as the council hall. With the help of two members of Bandhu – the NGO that had invited Bablu – they set up three tables and assembled the machines. By this time a crowd had gathered in the courtyard, looking at Bablu's contraptions curiously.

Bablu did a demonstration for the gathering, explaining the cost of the product, the working of the machine and how soon they could turn a profit. In Bihar, he had learned that when he tried to talk to his audience about hygiene and health, he lost their attention. But profit and loss always interested everyone.

Harish Negi, the rice trader, was the first to

put his hand up, wanting to examine the machine further before placing his bid. Bablu said, 'Bhai, this product is for women and will be made by them. I am selling my machine at low rates only if it will benefit and provide a livelihood for women.'

The words echoed in the courtyard. They were so simple but they held a promise of revolution. After a few minutes of disconcerting silence, a woman standing at the back, with a bruised face and a grubby child by her side, tentatively put her hand up.

Asha Rani Nautiyal bought the machine by giving Bablu the pieces of gold she had – a pair of flower-shaped earrings and a small nose pin that had belonged to her grandmother. Still falling short of the asking price, she threw in two goats and a hen and sealed the deal.

It was a leap into an unknown abyss for her, but then she was standing on the precipice of a cliff that was crumbling under her feet.

Prashant followed Bablu everywhere with his camera, a writing pad and a pen that never stopped moving those few weeks. He meticulously documented how Bablu helped Asha Rani set up a small unit, enlisting Mrs Mehta from Bandhu to help with distribution in the nearby villages, before Bablu and he took the train back to Indore.

20

Looking out of the window at the pouring rain, Sarita was grateful that she had to just go three floors down for their neighbour Manisha's baby shower. But first she had to finish a class and prepare the lunch boxes that Maina and she would carry the next morning.

She entered the minuscule kitchen, giving Maina a glass of milk. Putting the rice to boil in a stainless steel pot on one burner, she began dicing the onion and eggplant. Leaving the vegetables to gently cook and meld with all the spices, she wiped the sticky milk moustache off Maina's mouth and quickly dressed her in a green salwar kameez – though Maina had almost outgrown the salwar, it was nothing that tying the drawstring below the navel would not fix – and arranged her hair in a simple braid.

Heading back to the kitchen, Sarita added some tomatoes and water to the pan. Leaving the curry to simmer, she swiftly began draping her magenta silk sari with embroidered peacocks around her thin frame.

Creating six straight-edged pleats meticulously, she draped the fabric over her shoulder and pinned the sari to the blouse and petticoat with silver safety pins. She was contentedly humming an old Hindi song, while occasionally checking on her curry, when the doorbell rang.

Bablu Kewat was standing in the doorway. In the months that he had been coming to her for English lessons, she had always been dressed in a simple salwar kameez, her wavy hair in a single plait and her reading glasses firmly perched on her nose, or sometimes pushed on her head like a hairband.

Seeing her dressed in a sari, he blurted out in his still tottering English, 'Sarita ji, I went out of town for some days and you are fully changed. Very tip-top today. You are looking very nice.'

Sarita replied with a frown, 'Prabhash, this isn't quite right.' Bablu felt his cheeks flush with embarrassment, worried that perhaps he had been too forward. Then she laughed, 'Where do I even begin with the "fully changed" and "tip-top" bits? But I must say that the "You are looking very nice" part was perfect.'

And just like that his lessons had begun before he had even entered the shabby apartment.

21

The whirring fan sent a cold draught of the winter air towards Bablu, who was sitting on a lumpy couch in the living room of a one-bedroom flat that he now rented near Jhanda Chowk. Balancing a plate of congealing mattar paneer and cold chapattis on his bare legs, with Choti nestled beside him, he thought of Sarita Jagpal as he had frequently done in the last few months. His mind lingered on the way she always said his name, 'Prabhash'.

No woman had ever called him by his first name. He was Bablu to his family and the people he had grown up with in Mohana. Even Gowri had never used his name. She had always called him Suno ji, a term that meant are you listening, but used by all the women in the community to call out to their husbands.

It was a practice that had no constructive usage aside from creating mass confusion in crowded markets when a woman sharply hissed, 'Suno ji, enough! Stop that nonsense right now!' And fifteen startled men fearfully dropped what they were doing before realizing it was some other 'Suno ji' that was the target of that scathing tongue.

For a man as lonely as Bablu, whom every female member in his life had forsaken except for the pet sitting by his leg, the utterance of his name was enough to stir up deep emotions. Emotions that he had locked inside an unused part of his mind, securing the lid so firmly that their sour smell would not reach him.

But Sarita and her gently mocking voice, with her intelligence and independence, and the trace of uncertainty underneath, had seeped into those deep, dank parts of his self.

It had happened slowly. Bablu hadn't even realized it until he had returned from Uttarakhand.

A few months ago, Sarita, seeing him trying to hail an autorickshaw after class, had offered to drop him as far as the vegetable market as she was going in that direction too.

Sitting behind her on the scooter that balmy evening, he had been careful to tightly grip the metal handrail at the back. He did not want to make her uncomfortable by jostling against her when the scooter went into the numerous potholes that lent Hathipala Road the distinctive appearance of belonging to the lunar surface.

They spoke little during the ride, their words often cut off by the loud tooting of horns from homeward-bound commuters. Bablu, not wanting Sarita to spot him inadvertently looking at her in the rear-view mirror, kept his gaze on the thin electricity wires running across poles, drooping over newly patched roofs, criss-crossing the minaret of an old mosque, like a fine fishnet in the sky.

He was keenly aware of the woman sitting in the driver's seat, her smell, her hair. The squawking crows perched on the lines seemed to be watching him as well, judging him, causing an uneasy flip of his heart that he only days later identified as guilt.

He got off along with her at the market, buying tomatoes, okra and cauliflower, things he did not need, relishing walking beside her as she swung her rapidly filling plastic bag between them.

Sarita pointed out a billboard on the side of the road. It was a picture of a bespectacled man, in a purple shirt, holding his hand out and apparently counting on his fingers. 'Arvind's English and Mathematics' proclaimed the bold letters on the billboard and a quote seemingly from Mr Arvind himself stated, 'My students say that I am the father of fingering and formula.' This informative sentence was followed by a phone number and a small blurb – 'The one and only in the world'.

Sarita laughed. 'Be glad that you didn't join this class, Prabhash. Anything passes for English these days, really! I was lucky that I went to Sacred Heart Convent school where at least the teachers had decent grammar skills that made up for their heavy Punjabi twang.'

And she told him about growing up in Ludhiana, where her love for academics and reading was never understood by her family. Reminiscing with a distant smile on her face, she added, 'In Punjab all that we are meant to do is eat and drink. My parents thought books were meant only to be thrown into the bonfire at Lohri.'

She told him a funny story about her uncle Jippy, who once leaped over the Lohri bonfire tipsily, with the minor inconvenience of having set his kurta on fire. His brother-in-law then tried to douse the fire by upending the glass of whisky in his hand over the burning kurta sleeve.

But she said nothing about an absent husband or how she ended up in Indore and he didn't ask. He in return, ignoring her protests that he should only speak in English in order to practice, reminded her that class was now over, and switched to his impeccable Hindi.

He told her about his trip to Uttarakhand, meeting Prat Bhai on the train, about Asha Rani and her goats. 'You know, Sarita ji, the more I travel around the country, the bigger my dreams get,' he said. 'I want to install vending machines in schools all over the country. There are lakhs of young girls who start missing school once they begin menstruating. So many of them drop out altogether. I want to see them all finish their studies and enter the workforce, let them start making something of their lives, rather than just making dal and curry for the rest of their days.'

Sarita nimbly skipped over a large pile of cow dung on the pavement and replied, 'You reminded me of something, Prabhash. Many years ago, at my cousin Jasminder's wedding, eunuchs had come outside her house to give their blessings and of course extract a hefty sum for the same. I will never forget the words the elderly hijra sang, "Once he puts a garland over her head, the good wife has to stay in the kitchen and cut onions till she is dead." And the younger eunuchs danced to this, making graceful turns in their bright saris.

'\Of course, after three more songs when Jasminder's father refused to pay them, all that grace disappeared and one of the eunuchs lifted up her sari waist high and flashed him right in the face.'

Bablu laughed. 'It has happened to me too, at a traffic signal. I had no place to hide my face nor could I roll up a window!'

'Why?' asked Sarita.

Bablu laughed. 'Because I was on my cycle, Sarita ji.'

They walked to a small tea stall and sat down on the stained wooden benches. Sarita, holding her glass of milky tea in one hand and waving flies away with the other, kept glancing at Bablu. His face was only half visible under the shadow of the tin roof. He had such calm brown eyes and an uncomplicated gaze that he seemed to be largely focusing on the dented aluminium table between them.

He was one of the few men she had met who looked at women not as objects to be slotted in their place, or as beings that only existed to do their bidding.

Women have been looking for a cape and have been handed an apron for centuries. But here was a man who wanted to help women swing their apron around, let it flutter down their backs and watch them soar through the clear blue skies.

22

Prashant Batra submitted his story to the *Guardian* titled 'The first man to wear a sanitary napkin'. It was a four-page article chronicling Bablu Kewat's journey from Mohana to Indore. And with that, troops of ruddy-faced journalists wielding straw hats and bottled water along with their dictaphones began descending on Bablu Kewat's workshop from all over the world.

The *Times of India* was the first Indian newspaper to feature Bablu Kewat and his unique invention. A half-page story on page six, sandwiched between an advertisement for Sintex water storage tanks and an announcement that wished Sardar Ranga Singh a 'Very Jolly Birthday Sir ji'. Bablu Kewat had started getting famous.

There were television interviews where poker-faced anchors not quite focusing on the work he was doing with non-profit and women's groups kept trying to draw out salacious details of him wearing a pad and leaking blood all over himself.

He was invited to speak at universities and companies and conferences across the country. Bablu found himself enjoying these talks.

There was one rather memorable experience in Bhopal. It was a packed hall, with a panel of dignitaries from around the world and attended by the Minister of Commerce, Industry and Employment.

Bablu began his talk by pulling out a sanitary napkin from his pocket and waving it in front of the startled guests asking, 'How many men here have touched a sanitary pad in their life?'

When no one responded, he walked up to the minister and said, 'Well sir, here is your chance, come hold this, I promise it won't bite.' The startled minister looked helplessly around, waiting for someone to rescue him and, with no escape in sight, gingerly took the sanitary pad in his hand.

Bablu continued, 'You're feeling embarrassed holding that pad, aren't you, sir? This shame in discussing menstruation, in holding a sanitary pad, is one of the biggest hurdles we face. It is as if menstruation is not a natural function, but a sin that women unwillingly commit through their uterus and have to hide away from prying eyes, lest they be declared guilty of the crime of bleeding.

'This shame is the reason why women take their stained pieces of cloth, wash them secretively and hang them to dry in places where even the rays of the sun cannot spot them. Then they end up using those mouldy, bacteria-laden pieces of fabric, and get diseases. Let us all refuse to be part of this game of shame because it is nothing but a losing game for all humanity.'

The audience was spellbound and couldn't stop clapping. Taking his sanitary pad back from the hapless minister's hands, Bablu added with a twinkle in his eye, 'And I would like to end my speech by thanking women and their menstrual cycles. Without them, this talk, along with our very existence, would not be possible.'

Later, laughing about the event, he confessed to Sarita, 'Sarita ji, I told them only ten per cent of women in India used a sanitary pad. Actually I

fudged the number. It is only five per cent. I just
added five per cent more on stage because I did
not want to embarrass Bharat Mata so much in
front of all foreigners.'

23

One evening, over cups of tea, Bablu was entertaining Professor Sharma with his most recent adventures as a sanitary napkin salesman. Wherever he went, he encountered so many interesting characters, and he hoarded up the stories to tell the professor and Sarita.

He recounted a tale about a woman in Chhattisgarh who refused to switch from her dirty rags to the pads because she explained, 'If a dog gets hold of the menstrual pad and runs on the street, that's a sign that my mother-in-law will die.'

'She refused to listen to me,' Bablu said, 'even though I tried explaining that if that were true, then millions of women all over India would deliberately throw their sanitary pads on the streets, hoping for dogs to carry them off.'

Professor Sharma laughed while Bablu, biting into one of the bhajiyas Mrs Sharma had prepared, said, 'These moong dal bhajiyas are almost as good as the ones Ma used to make.'

He hadn't thought about his mother in a while and this sudden memory of her robbed him briefly of words. Professor Sharma, sensing his mood shift, gently broached the topic of Bablu reuniting with his family.

Bablu turned away and looking at Choti playing on the lawn he said, 'Whenever I think of them, my heart feels heavy. They all abandoned me. Since the time I was fourteen I had sacrificed everything for my mother and my sisters and when the time came to stand by me, they all fled.'

Professor Sharma asked, 'And what about Gowri?'

Bablu replied, 'My mother thought Gowri was the right woman for me and once she was in my life I tried to be the right man for her but marriage is about understanding, Professor saab, and where did she ever understand me?

'You know, soon after she left, her brother came to see me. We were standing on the porch and he called me all sorts of names. The neighbours gathered and then he pushed me down the stairs and left. What had I ever done to deserve all this humiliation? I do not want to turn around and choke on the dust of my footsteps, Professor saab. Now the only path for me lies ahead.'

24

On a rain-filled evening, sitting across Sarita's dining table, his head bent over grammar textbooks meant for sixth graders, in his idiosyncratic English, Bablu said, 'I got mail, Sarita ji, from Unilever. They are calling me to London and saying to give a talk in front of their top managers about how I am making sanitary pads in such cheap way.

'I don't know how I will talk in English and all properly, little worry in my heart.' And then he laughed, adding, 'Sarita ji, when I told to Sanjay, my neighbour on second floor, that I may be going to London next month so can he giving Choti food and take her walking, he said, "No, no, Kewat don't go, even Bruce Lee was poisoned by these British people!"'

Sarita leaned across the table and, putting her hand over his, said, 'Prabhash, I don't know if the British poisoned Bruce Lee, but I am pretty sure that you will not be poisoned at the Unilever event, unless you decide to chew on their Lifebuoy soap.

'Go and don't worry about speaking on stage. It doesn't matter if your English is incorrect. If you feel more comfortable, just speak in Hindi. Remember all these people, these MBAs, are calling you on stage because they know that despite all their education, you are more brilliant than them. After all, it is you who have set up more than two hundred sanitary napkin manufacturing units in seven states, as you never tire of telling me – not them. It is they who need to learn something from you.'

Not long after, Bablu Kewat, with freshly oiled hair, a new pair of grey trousers, a mustard sleeveless Nehru jacket and his new Bata shoes, stood in line at the airport waiting for his boarding pass. The woman with immaculate red lipstick across the counter asked, 'Sir, what would you prefer, window or aisle?'

Not quite understanding the question, he

nonchalantly replied, 'I already have Windows on my laptop so I will take the aisle.'

Bablu Kewat had a comfortable journey in his aisle seat to Heathrow. And at the Unilever convention the next day, remembering Sarita's words, he delivered a simple speech about both his journey and his beliefs.

He ended his talk by saying, 'Big business is like a mosquito, a parasite. It can make society ill. My method of business is like a bee. You take nectar from the flower while benefiting the system.' And then looking directly at his audience of executives with degrees from Harvard and Yale he ended his speech, gently challenging them, 'I classify people into three categories, uneducated, a little educated and surplus educated. A little educated man like me has done this. Surplus educated people, what are you going to do for society?'

The applause didn't stop. Bablu stood on the stage, his heart bursting with pride, as the solitary spotlight focused on him. He wished he could share this moment with someone. He thought about his parents. They should have been here. His poor father, who had not gone further than the perimeter of Mohana, and his mother, who had travelled just a bit further, to Dewas, cooking in different homes, trying to raise three children.

The hurt he had nursed against his mother faded. He suddenly realized, as he stood alone on the stage, that he was not here despite his mother, but because of her. Growing up, seeing her struggling for her family's survival and her indomitable strength that seemed to deal with every obstacle had made him see women in a role different from the customary one.

His journey had begun as a young boy when he decided to drop out of school to help his mother. The lessons he had learned during that time, the understanding he gained, all had their role in bringing him here, to this very auditorium. The yearning for his family, deeply buried in his heart, returned to him with all the sharpness of a fresh wound.

After the conference, Bablu spent the rest of his trip riding the open red bus, seeing all the tourist spots of London, the Big Ben, the Tower Bridge, standing at the gates of Buckingham Palace and walking at length around Hyde Park till he got a dreadful shoe bite.

Then he headed back home but not before he bought a purse emblazoned with the Union Jack and a matching keychain for Sarita, and an 'I love London' T-shirt for Maina.

25

Ropes of marigold flowers were hung in sweeping loops across the entrance of Bablu Kewat's office. A pandit in a white dhoti was sitting on the floor, arranging numerous idols of gods and goddesses on a silk-covered platform, decorating it with fruits and rice grains in intricate patterns, waiting to add the book of accounts which would also be duly anointed with a sacred red dot and placed at the altar.

Bablu had a lot to thank God for this year. In January he had been the recipient of one of the highest awards given to civilians by the Government of India, the Padma Shri, and he had also been commissioned by the chief minister of Bihar to help set up over a hundred sanitary pad making units in the state.

Distributing Diwali bonuses along with packets of sweets to his workers, Bablu was waiting to finish the ceremony and head to Sarita's house. He had purchased fireworks for Maina – sparklers, Lakshmi bombs and rockets that would go high into the sky before bursting into an array of dazzling stars.

The telephone on his desk rang and Bablu picked up the cordless phone, clamping it between his ear and shoulder as he lifted yet another gift-wrapped box of sweets. At the other end, a hesitant voice said, 'Hello? It's me.' And with a nervous laugh she added, 'Do you still remember me?'

Bablu felt a nerve twitch from his shoulder to his forearm, his throat went dry and he set the box of sweets on the table, walking towards a quieter corner of the office.

There was only one appropriate reply that he could give. With a heart filled with an ache that was both sweet and sour, like a half-ripened mango, still green on the other side, he said, 'It is not so easy for a man to forget his wife.'

~

The night sky was filled with fireworks as the city celebrated Diwali. Sounds of excited voices and laughter rang all around him but Bablu Kewat felt hollow as he stood next to Sarita.

He watched Maina make small circles with the sparklers in the dark and saw the warmth in Sarita's eyes when he helped Maina put a rocket inside a glass bottle and lit the wick for her as she gleefully watched it zigzag into the sky.

Later that evening, with the exhausted child asleep on the couch, he sat at the same chipped wooden table where it had all begun and told Sarita about the conversation with his wife. Gowri had told him that she had been looking for him unsuccessfully till someone sent her a magazine that featured an article on him along with a phone number for Kewat Industries.

Bablu had felt numb through the conversation. As his wife spoke, Sarita's face had loomed in his mind. He didn't know what to feel. And then there was a pause, a few muffled sounds of the phone being handed over and, as he heard his mother's voice, Bablu had finally broken down.

26

The jeep hurtled down the dusty road from Dewas to Mohana, with Bablu holding the steering wheel with one hand and now and then patting Choti with the other. The dog was sitting in the front seat, barking occasionally, her tail wagging and her head hanging out of the window, perhaps catching traces of long-forgotten trails.

Bablu was returning home but it had not been an easy decision. Since Gowri's phone call, Bablu felt there was a flickering tube light in his head, going on and off, on and off.

He oscillated between dread and wistful yearning. He had deep misgivings, a fear of being contained in a coop he had possibly outgrown, as he relived the past again and again.

Then the tube light flickered on and he could

see himself sitting on the stairs with his mother as she rubbed coconut oil into his hair on Sunday mornings, and images of sticky faces and mouths filled with pink candy floss, gleaming in the sunlight as he walked back with his sisters from the local fair.

And Gowri, lying down next to him in the dark, her long hair sprawled over the pillow, her red bindi, as smudged as the kohl around her eyes, turning towards him and giggling at a now long-forgotten jest. But then the tube light would flicker off and he would return to those dark days of being alone, ostracized, abandoned.

Finally he had gone to meet Professor Sharma. Walking around the lawn, throwing a half-chewed yellow ball for Choti, Professor Sharma said, 'Bablu, relationships may tear but they are not clothes where you throw out a ripped shirt and replace it with a new one. A principled man must try to stitch together his bonds carefully, time and again.'

Professor Sharma waved towards the porch where Mrs Sharma was sitting with her crochet and said, 'Look at me, Bablu, I will be wearing my shirt, faded and patched but softened with time, till the day I eventually fade away myself.'

Bablu went to Sarita's house later that evening. They sat across the table, separated it seemed by a world rather than a piece of wood. He found it difficult to look into her eyes, eyes that suddenly looked weary, with desolation lingering at their edges.

Close to breaking point himself, he continued, 'Sarita ji, I thought my rickshaw was empty, I had travelled such a long way, a distance measured not just in kilometres but in time itself, hours, days, years where nothing was visible, even in the rear-view mirror. But I didn't realize that the meter had stayed down and the passenger who had stepped out could just as easily step back in. I have to go back, Sarita ji, back to her, my mother and my town.'

Sarita did not say a word, though her pain was evident – in her hand that trembled slightly as she sat still covering her mouth, in her rigidly held neck as she kept her gaze fixed on the table between them. She then nodded once, almost imperceptibly, and walked him to the door.

A week after that Bablu packed up his life in Indore, loaded his jeep and here he was, six years and forty-seven kilometres later.

He could see his house up ahead with the electricity pole outside, where he used to tether his cycle, though time had diminished the gleam of fresh paint on the exterior. Bablu also noticed a horde of people gathered at the gate with overstretched smiles and garlands in hand. They were waiting for him as if he was a visiting minister distributing free televisions a day before voting begins.

He parked on the side and walked towards them, spotting his family, half hidden by the crowd.

But before he could reach them, there were raucous cheers and people rushing to put their garlands around his neck.

The headman, who had once decided to hang him upside down from a tree, clasped him to his chest saying, 'Beta, I always told everyone, Bablu Kewat's grandfather was a very intelligent man and that boy has gone on his Dada ji, he will be world famous one day.'

Parul's husband, Mahesh, held Bablu's hand – flipping over his palm, he traced a line on it and, displaying his sudden knowledge of palmistry, turned to his beaming wife, declaring, 'See, didn't I tell you, Parul, this boy has a luck line that sweeps across his entire palm, he was always destined to be a great man, I have been saying this since he was a child.'

He saw Akram standing behind Ganjkaran and walked up to him, squeezing his friend's shoulder affectionately while Ganjkaran droned on, 'Kewat saab, I still remember the day you came to me and bought sanitary pads, many reporters had come to interview us and I told them that I knew right at that moment our Kewat saab was a genius type of person.'

Bablu made his way through the crowd, towards his family, touched his sobbing mother's feet as he always had when greeting her, hugged his nephew, who sported a pubescent moustache and pimples now, and his sisters. Gowri was standing in a corner, an uncertain smile fluttering on her lips. She looked both frightened and hopeful. He took her by the hand and entered his home.

27

Sonal nestled on the front seat of the jeep, her small head leaning against the window as she played with her Rubik's Cube. 'How much further, Papa?' she asked. Bablu looked at his ten-year-old daughter and replied, 'Almost there, Sona, another ten minutes.'

Gowri did not understand the point of these excursions that the father and daughter embarked upon ever so often, just like she didn't understand why when he could sell his machines for a greater profit, he didn't. Why they could not move to a better house, or get a new car.

Rachna of course had her own ideas, that he was pretending to live a modest life while squirrelling all his money into Swiss bank accounts. She was convinced that his frequent trips to Europe to give lectures were just a cover-up for his unscrupulous activities. But Bablu had stopped explaining himself a long time ago.

Sonal, having solved her cube many times and still unable to beat her best time of forty-three seconds, started toying with the threaded lime and chilli that Bablu had hung on the rear-view mirror. Tapping it like a ball and watching it sway, she said, 'Papa, isn't this meant to keep the evil eye away? But you always say not to believe in superstitions, then why do you hang it?'

Bablu was silent. It was not a superstition but a souvenir from his past, a flashlight illuminating a single moment, in a mind crowded with dusty memories. A fragile soap bubble filled with images of sitting pillion behind a remarkable woman on her scooter, dodging potholes. Her stopping at a traffic light, buying a cotton thread with lime and chilli from a street vendor, laughing as she said, 'In English there is a saying "when life gives you lemons, you make lemonade". But in India when life gives us lemons, we turn them into talismans threaded with chillies to protect us from the bumpy roads it takes us on.'

Unable to tell his daughter about a life spent making difficult choices, he said instead, 'Some superstitions are based on science – the juice from the lime and chilli keeps pests away. It is a simple insecticide.'

Bablu parked the jeep at the edge of the Kheoni wildlife sanctuary and, holding his daughter's hand, walked into the woods, where he would show her how to pick the right stones to rub together and make a fire, point out the monkeys taking calculated leaps as they jumped from branch to branch, the disciplined black ants marching in a straight line like soldiers in a parade, and the brown butterflies delicately sitting on wildflowers, feeding without destroying.

This fictionalized story is based on Arunachalam Muruganantham and his marvellous invention, the low cost sanitary pad making machine. All characters, places and incidents, however, are the author's own creation.

Acknowledgements

I would like to thank Padma Shri Arunachalam Muruganantham or Muruga as I call him, not just because my tongue trips over his name, but because he is also now a friend. Muruga is the inventor of the low cost sanitary pad making machine and a social entrepreneur who works tirelessly to remove the taboos around menstruation.

I had to chase him for months before he finally agreed to meet me and then, after lengthy interviews, gave me permission to fictionalize his story for this book.

A hug to Aarav and Nitara, for bearing with me and leaving me alone with my computer whenever I yelped, 'Don't come close, there are insects on my desk!' This was not an absolute falsehood because during the last monsoon season we did have a bug infestation and I spent hours at my computer, typing with one hand while scratching my legs with the other.

Merliyn Joseph, you amazing woman, I owe you one for patiently answering all my queries about Amma and meen moilee and for the time I interrupted you in the middle of a movie and asked, 'So when you die, which cemetery are you likely to be buried in?'

To my wonderful Mom, I am not half the woman you are but even that half seems to be enough.

Rinke Khanna, may we both grow old like Noni Appa and Binni. There is so much of us that went into dreaming up those two sisters.

A hug to my Nani for dragging me to the Jamatkhana for so many years.

A big thank you to the fabulous Jaishree Ram Mohan, Gavin Morris, Rachna Kalra, Harsimran Gill, Anish Chandy, Sonali Zohra and the great team at Juggernaut Books for making it all happen.

Chiki Sarkar, my wonderful publisher and editor, once again, I could not have done this without you.

A Note on the Author

Twinkle Khanna is an acclaimed columnist and the bestselling author of *Mrs Funnybones*. She lives in Mumbai.

1

CRAFTED FOR MOBILE READING

Thought you would never read a book on mobile? Let us prove you wrong.

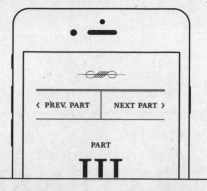

Beautiful Typography

The quality of print transferred
to your mobile. Forget ugly PDFs.

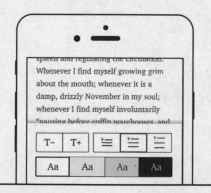

Customizable Reading

Read in the font size, spacing
and background of your liking.

AN EXTENSIVE LIBRARY

Including fresh, new, original Juggernaut
books from the likes of Sunny Leone, Praveen
Swami, Husain Haqqani, Umera Ahmed,
Rujuta Diwekar and lots more. Plus, books
from partner publishers and loads of free
classics. Whichever genre you like, there's
a book waiting for you.

3

DON'T JUST READ; INTERACT

We're changing the reading experience from passive to active.

Ask authors questions

Get all your answers from the horse's mouth.
Juggernaut authors actually reply to every
question they can.

***

Rate and review

Let everyone know of your favourite reads or
critique the finer points of a book – you will be
heard in a community of like-minded readers.

***

Gift books to friends

For a book-lover, there's no nicer gift than
a book personally picked. You can even
do it anonymously if you like.

***

Enjoy new book formats

Discover serials released in parts over
time, picture books including comics,
and story-bundles at discounted rates.
And coming soon, audiobooks.

4

LOWEST PRICES & ONE-TAP BUYING

Books start at ₹10 with regular discounts and free previews.

Paytm Wallet, Cards
& Apple Payments

On Android, just add a Paytm Wallet once and
buy any book with one tap. On iOS, pay with one
tap with your iTunes-linked debit/credit card.

Click the QR Code with a QR scanner app
or type the link into the Internet browser
on your phone to download the app.

ANDROID APP

bit.ly/juggernautandroid

iOS APP

bit.ly/juggernautios

For our complete catalogue, visit www.juggernaut.in
To submit your book, send a synopsis and two
sample chapters to books@juggernaut.in
For all other queries, write to contact@juggernaut.in